The Pool

Richard Collis

Published in 2022 by Discover Your Bounce
Publishing

www.discoveryourbouncepublishing.com

ISBN 978-1-914428-12-8

Page design and typesetting by Discover Your
Bounce Publishing

PROLOGUE

The young boy trotted excitedly at his father's side. Ahead of them a wooden hut jutted out from the reinforced bankside over the pool. Great trees surrounded it, but the water level had diminished substantially in recent times. Nevertheless, the water still sat motionless, basking in the early morning sun, exemplifying tranquillity. The boy freed himself from his father's hand and ran on, bringing an appreciative smile to the older man's face; my son, he thought, and followed the boy.

When he reached the shack, the child was standing on a bench looking out of the open front across the scene. He felt no need to chastise his son for being too close to the edge, but laid a protective hand on his shoulder.

"Beautiful, isn't it." He smiled. The boy said nothing. Awe had struck him, and he knew in his young heart that this place was somehow magical, somehow important, somehow his.

"There is a myth that says a young lady drowned here many, many years ago," said the father, wanting to fuel his son's imagination ever further.

"What else?" replied the boy, his eyes never faltering from the view in front.

"What do you mean, 'what else'?"

"What other stories are there?"

"About this pool?"

"Yes."

"None that I know of, I'm afraid," said the older man. "Nothing else has happened here."

There was a pause.

"No Daddy, you're wrong," said the boy, unmoving. "Lots has happened here. You just don't see it."

The pool was silent. The soft breeze brushed across its surface, occasionally sending the floating lilies colliding into one another; the water itself remained untouched by the faint breath, as if Nature itself wished for it to remain that way. Only the rain could touch it, diving hard onto the surface and sending small diamonds of water up in response; small rainbows of colour refracting across the pool. Here was Nature at play, shielded from the extremities by the parenting hands of the trees; the Gods having given these great arms of ash, elm and willow the job of protecting so sacred a plot. They provided an almost green shield around the pool, hiding it from view, until, when parted, the magic of the scene could be released.

In times gone past the pool had been integral to the ritual cleansing of the body and soul, or as a place of worship to the Gods. The still waters, so naturally clear and blue, were sacred, as if the Gods themselves would stop there to refresh their weary bodies after a long journey or great toil. Even the babies and heirs of great kings and queens were given their first bath in the waters of the silent pool, so akin was it to Nature. So blessed was the water, so steeped in faith and reverence, so was its belief.

But few had experienced that magic for many years.

And with time comes great change.

CHAPTER 1

FENWOOD

Looking down from the tree-covered slopes, the city of Fenwood appeared nothing more than a vast sea of wooden shacks packed close together. The smoke from each chimney entwined and floated away in the wind down the valley created by the North and South Downs on either side. The dwellings were made from the wood of the neighbouring birch trees; trees that were happy to be felled to house the folk that cared much, and toiled hard, for the natural world around them. Great areas of forest ran untouched and free throughout the valley. Hedgerows, home to many animals, were unspoiled, used as dividing borders between fields set aside for farming maize, hops, barley and sunflowers (the seeds of which formed a substantial ingredient for many of the local dishes). Other fields allowed the livestock, predominantly cattle, to roam free without danger of being poached or attacked as all the farming land was owned by the city, with the profits and workload shared equally between the workers.

It was somewhat dumbfounding to say that Fenwood was a city; the nature of the buildings, the size of the dwelling area and the habitual running had very much the essence of a village. Yet within its boundaries, away and separate from the dwellings and immediate fields, rising behind the brilliance of the dancing sunflowers, the single stone gleaming towers and ramparts stood proud. Fenwood, being the only inhabited part of the Downs region, was therefore the principal city, home to the High Priest, Master Craftsmen, Elders and High Family. Within the walls of the shimmering white stone castle, closed off from the public, dwelt the Queen of Fenwood, her closest subjects and advisors, and her only daughter: Ivy.

Ivy led, even in relation to the cut-off settlement around her, a very sheltered life. Her days were filled with the steady echo of following footsteps or the weight of watching eyes. She was the only remaining life and hope of the castle and had to be protected. Her brothers, seven in total, had all been taken from the world before their seventh birthdays. With each early death hope had

diminished just a little more. Ivy had been something of a
miracle. The Queen was approaching her sixtieth year,
with no memory of a conception, when the bewildered
medic (himself well into his nineties) announced her to be
with child. It was upon this moment that the long-
whispered loving name 'Mother' was adopted, within the
city, for the Queen.

Ivy was born the day spring broke in Fenwood,
creating as good a reason as any for the city dwellers to
revel in a week-long festival of ale, tobacco and carnival.
The baby had been paraded around, blessed on all sides
and drunk to, before being invested as a Child of the
Valley, a ritual that made every child equal in the eyes of
the Gods (naturally the common city folk were expected,
and willingly obliged, to ignore the hypocrisy of such a
situation). Thus was the way of Fenwood, and Ivy was free
to wander the streets and fields, albeit under the watchful
gaze of her minders, in particular her devoted servant
Laurent.

At sixteen, Ivy was, as princesses should be and often
are in stories, very beautiful. Her long, shimmering brown
hair hung in waves over her slender shoulders, whilst her
delicate green eyes ever wondered at the beauty of the
world around her. On her many long walks across the
fields (but never beyond the borders of the Downs),

Laurent was her constant companion. Laurent's young eyes were equally naïve and wondrous, but he had not been blessed with the same beauty as Ivy. Upon his face lay the pock-scars of a disease he had narrowly survived in infancy, and thus could never be loved by Ivy in the way that her every essence dominated his crippled heart. She never saw the glances and glimpses he cast her way, with her eyes always looking around her at the wonders of the natural world. His charm flowed through his words, falling like velvet onto the ears of the listener. Ivy kept him as a close servant, and friend, for his command of language, his ability to conjure wonders with his conversation, and for his infallible loyalty, like that of a brother.

*   *   *

Alone in her chamber, the Queen pulled back her long, silver hair into a hasty knot, screwing up her nose in the mirror at its straw-like texture. Despite her glowing complexion, the wrinkles on her face reminded her sharply that she was ageing.

"It will soon be time," she muttered, but knew immediately that she was lying to herself. Lifting a dark purple liquid to her mouth she sipped slowly, allowing it to coat and soothe her throat. A voice from outside the door sounded, nervously.

"Mother? Er, Ma'am? Did you call?"

The Queen shook her head with a smile of awareness.

"No, Maria," she replied softly. Then added, "Have you seen my daughter?" She waited as clearly the lady-in-waiting asked the other servants who were gathered dutifully outside the door.

"She was last seen with Laurent, walking the herb garden to the East side of the castle. Shall we fetch her?"

"No, thank you." The Queen gazed thoughtfully into the mirror. "I will be out soon." She let out a sigh. Call Ivy? What would she say to her daughter? Running her lined and knotted hands over the dressing table she pulled out the spidery scrawl of Ernest's written reminder: 'Mid-Morning, Apple Ale tasting'. The young princess would not be needed for this morning's gala anyway.

Hops (not his real name, but adopted by the city as many could not pronounce that which he had been born with), the landlord of the Oak and Maize Inn, loaded the last of the solid wood flagons onto his cart. He felt immense pride that his home-brewed Apple Ale was to be sampled by the Queen at this morning's produce testing. He smiled and waved at several passersby, exchanging pleasantries and humbly informing them why he was dressed for ceremony and locking the inn door.

"Mother has requested my attendance this morning Mr Heathers. That Apple Ale you drank and enjoyed yesternight? She shall be partaking of it this morning!"

"Will she manage a whole orchard's worth, I wonder?" came the jovial response from Mr Heathers' companion.

"Ha, no, I do not believe she will enjoy it in quite such a quantity as you, my good sir!" chuckled Hops.

"And will you be open later today?" interjected a red-nosed lady, who had eavesdropped on the exchange.

"Very much so Mrs Flax. I'll make sure I have some of the damson wine cooled, just for you."

Hops' inn was flourishing. People used the inns in Fenwood as social gathering areas, not necessarily for consuming great amounts of mead, ale, and fruit wines, but to meet with friends and neighbours. They played simple hand-carved wooden board games and caught up with the news of the locality; there was little concern for what happened beyond the borders. Stories and worldly updates came down the journey-ways via the merchants and traders who arrived on market days to sell their wares. These were listened to, but generally held in as much tangible regard as a folk story that parents would tell their children. Record-keepers kept their own histories of the events of Fenwood, both statistical and folklore, that were available for public viewing yet seldom busied over.

The history of Fenwood flowed through its traditions, ceremonies and rituals. From the stories that were told, running strongly through everyday life, resounding in the reverence of the land and the Gods who blessed the people and very world around them. At the centre of the tales, and of Fenwood itself, stood the ruling families and their home, an impressive stone castle. It was clear to all who saw it that, despite being made of brilliant white stone, the castle was the oldest building in the outlying area, and the Downs region. Time and the weather had certainly made their impression on the stonework. Dark discolouration tainted patches, pocks were created from crumbling stone and, on sections of the walls, nature had been allowed to take its course, with ivy flourishing. Fenwood and the surrounding areas had never been affluent, only rich in land, timber and hard work, and so the stone that had been brought in serviced the entire castle: internal and external walls, stairs, basins and other constructed appliances.

This was no castle, however, that owed any inspiration from fortresses or great imposing ramparts and dungeon blocks. The palace of Fenwood was intended to house a sovereign of esteem and grandeur. The walls ran a rectangular shape with a turret at each corner, each declaring the flag of the monarch proudly and stationed with guards, more for ceremony than protection. Beneath the walls, inside the grounds, were rooms dedicated to clerics and other royalty-related professions: clothmakers, bookbinders and physicians. Each room was lit with vivid stained-glass windows whilst still decorated sparsely. At either end stood a large stone gateway with oaken doors, opening and closing on carefully crafted wooden hinges. Around the outside, the stonework had once been meticulously chiselled into white stone flowers, but now they too felt the effects of the weather. The doors themselves were seldom closed so that anyone could wander the beautiful gardens inside at their leisure, smelling the uniquely fragranced flowers or wondering at the finely trimmed and shaped hedges.

In the centre of the gardens stood the citadel; five layers stacked high, each layer proportioned smaller than the one beneath, like a stepped pyramid. The interior rooms were often simply decorated – a hanging tapestry or painted mural – allowing the white stone to dominate. Many of the corridors were poorly lit, with the larger windows being saved for the rooms, leaving the passages between them to linger in shadow. The larger windows were shaped and filled with leaded glass panels; stained glass was seldom used (except for in the regal rooms) so as not to detract from the fine woven tapestries. The royal rooms dominated the upper chambers, with the greatest of the weavings and carvings adorning the walls of chambers and corridors. The lower areas and halls were used as ceremonial and ritualistic rooms, ready to be decorated and dressed as required. All matters of castle life took place here: the kitchens, the banqueting, the ceremony, the day-to-day running and the seemingly never-ending silence and tradition.

Mr Kitterton, the Master of Ceremonies, stood upon a wooden frame, carefully hanging garlands of leaves and apples between two gurning 'goblinesque' busts. Removing his gloved hand slowly and carefully, he stepped down and smiled at his success in making the decoration hang. His wise face turned to a frown as he noticed the structures upon which his hand-crafted garland hung.

"I really hate those gargoyles," he muttered to himself in his light voice. However, his thoughts were broken by the arrival of a young boy, dressed in serving cloth.

"Mr…. Mr…. Ummm…" came the stumbling interruption.

"…Kitterton…" the old man offered.

"Yes." The boy could barely look up into his eyes. "Hops is on his way. I seen him pulling his cart by the tobacco shop." Pause. "Sir."

"I SAW him. Saw him," corrected Kitterton, with patience.

"You've already seen him too, sir?" The boy was taken aback.

"No, I'm merely… Never mind." Kitterton laid his hand on the boy's shoulder. "Run to Mrs Maltcross and let her know that breakfast is required, as well as the ceremonial food. Then fetch Ernest to me. Got that?" The boy nodded and left the room. Kitterton smiled at his keenness. Suddenly he realised that he still had three garlands to hang before running through the ceremony with the Queen. He looked again at the gargoyles and tutted.

CHAPTER 2

MORNING

Despite being governed somewhat by God-appeasing rituals and the cycle of the seasons, time was not something of great importance in Fenwood, being as there was plenty of it. The people of the city awoke when the cock crowed at the rising of the sun, and as soon as they were fed and watered met at the Meeting House for the issuing of the daily tasks. The day was then spent at toil - the men in the fields, and the women-folk set to cleaning, baking, caring for children, or indulging in crafts that could be sold at market. It was known that some women were so skilled in needlework or whittling that they could make substantial acts of trade based on the price people were willing to pay for rugs or ornaments to adorn their homes.

Even though the nature of the city was predominantly earthly, man-made material artefacts were highly regarded, especially when they depicted Gods or idols, or significant events in the history of the city. Of course, work of supreme quality and grandeur were often presented as gifts to the Queen and her family.

At the appearance of the moon in the day sky, the men retired from work and the labyrinthine city came to life. It was at this time when the shop-smiths did much of their trade. Reputable businessmen of the city had set up shops and workshops, and despite many dwellers doing jobs for themselves and the threat of competition, these men made a good living; among them were ironmongers, bakeries, dairy stores, bookmakers and fishmongers. Westwood's Bakery and Glanville's Dairy had passed down through the generations of their respective families, only changing location when a larger building was needed. Both now stood on either side of one of the larger streets leaving the marketplace, attracting custom even though Fenwood wives had long spent their time baking bread and making butter and cheese whilst their husbands worked in the fields.

It was some months after the local produce tasting and Fenwood life had continued as traditionally and uncomplicated as ever it had. The sun rose late one mid-autumn day, but the castle had sprung to life at the first crowing of the cockerel. It was vitally important that all be ready for when Mother and Ivy arose; not that they would be irate at having been kept waiting for breakfast or the Morning Report, but as a matter of general principle for Mrs Maltcross, the head of the kitchens. She was a gaunt looking lady, a skeleton draped casually in flesh, who could perhaps have benefitted from the over-exuberant meals she laid out (two-thirds of which would be wasted) four times a day: breakfast, lunch, dinner and supper. Mrs Maltcross never scolded or shouted at her kitchen staff, but nevertheless her air of rigidity prevented them from falling below her exceptional standards. Indeed, on the morning in question, all hands could be seen to be very busy at work, preparing the suckling pigs, fresh bread, eggs and fruit, not to mention other indulgent plates that would be arranged in front of the tiny stomachs of Mother and Ivy.

Mother lay in bed, grimacing at the prospect. She had not the heart to tell Mrs Maltcross that her stomach was in fact the same size as her small eyes, and that one was simply not ready to eat an entire suckling pig at that time of the morning. She rose slowly, her joints warming under the late morning sun and her long, fragile white hair falling to her back. A splutter escaped her lips, followed by another, and then a large, hacking rasp that made the Queen stumble forward. Guiding herself with a wrinkled hand along the furniture, she made her way towards the fresh air. From her window she could look out across the people – her people – and feel happy that the land she loved was safe in their hands. When the time came, Ivy would take her place in this chamber that overlooked Fenwood. The room itself was round and, unlike most of the rooms in the castle, the walls were not white (aside from the kitchen where they had long since yellowed and cracked in the smoke and changes of temperature). Instead, the brickwork was adorned with handcrafted tapestries from generations past, celebrating the beauty of the land around them, the regality of kings and queens, and the wonder of the Gods. The twine used had been dyed using juices from local fruits and berries, so each tapestry held a radiance of colour that was enough to illuminate the room, but also held the light from the leaf patterned chandelier that hung ceremoniously in the centre of the room. It was rumoured that the room had been built round so that no corners could cast shadows for anything unwholesome to hide in, at the request of King Crowstaff; a physically degenerate man whose every move was made in great fear of imminent death. Yet since the unsure early days of Fenwood (named after the surroundings) the royal families had grown as strong and secure as the ring of oaks that surrounded the city; until here stood Mother, proud, with an ageing beauty and unmistakable majesty. The ruler of the last remaining stronghold in the land. Yet as another cough barked from her quivering lips, she felt far from majestic and powerful.

Ivy had not yet risen. She had taken to waking and rising early so that she could meet Laurent for a pre-breakfast stroll to see the daybreak work of the city men. However, the book that she had started reading the previous night still held her attention past her normal sleeping hour. It was a history book of the land, a time before cities were stone and metal, and all stood very much like Fenwood: small wooden settlements surrounded by fields and forests. Ivy had visited these other cities with her mother on royal visits and the stone had made them cold, frightened and self-conscious. The kings and queens seemed as unwelcoming as the brickwork, and were surrounded by raven-like black-robed court advisors. She had shuddered at the prospect and lay the book down on her bedside cabinet, where it still lay now as the girl dreamt in comfort.

Laurent hovered nervously outside the door to Ivy's room, a small bell still ringing in his hand. He silenced it. She was either asleep or not in the room. Was it wise to enter without being called to do so? Laurent paused, but then the handle turned in his hand before he had a chance to think. The door opened silently, and he peered into the brilliant white room. She was asleep, a hazed picture of innocence behind the netting that hung between the four oaken posts around the bed. Laurent quivered as he moved towards the bed, his left eye flinching as he drew back the netting. She appeared to be smiling at him, and he felt like crying.

In her dream a shadow fell over the rose-arch on the forest path. Ivy shuddered and awoke.

The screams and crashing brought servants rushing from all quarters to find, startlingly, Ivy comforting a distressed Laurent. Her screams upon waking to his scarred face had shocked him further still, petrifying the frail mind and body that seemed unable to house such a calm and comforting voice. Ivy held his shaking hands in hers, and her nearness seemed to lessen the shaking to that of his regular demeanour.

"We're fine now, thank you," said Ivy, turning to the onlookers at the door. There was a chorus of "Yes m'lady," before the group dispersed. Only a young boy remained, a thin coating of flour on his person giving him an almost ghostlike quality.

"Can I help you, Alvin?" asked Ivy, somewhat at a loss to why Mrs Maltcross's son had remained.

"Breakfast's ready," squeaked the little boy.

"Thank you, Alvin," Ivy replied with a smile. The boy scurried off down the corridor in the general direction of the kitchen, leaving a small trail of flour on the greying floor.

*　　　　　*　　　　　*

High upon the Downs a small humanlike creature surveyed the settlement before its eyes. It longed to explore this new terrain; although something in its memory felt like it had seen this place before. It was wary and stayed still, so as not to be seen. Its skin had a weathered tan, but also a green hue that blended with its natural habitat. The hair was long, brown and wild; its eyes were piercingly green, moving quickly, always seeing, and very alive. Yet something in its nature had given it a sense of decency and a need for clothing, and a carefully tailored deerskin was wrapped around its lower hips. It was not hungry; it was not thirsty. It just waited.

*   *   *

Mother inhaled deeply and waited for the nausea to pass. The suckling pig, fresh from the spit, appeared to be grinning at her. She glanced over at her daughter, whose face had also drained somewhat of colour at the copious amount of food which had been laid in front of them for breakfast. It was the same every morning, but never ceased to unsettle the two ladies. The table, that seated thirty people, was half-filled with an array of silver platters of varying sizes, each representing the hard work of Mrs Maltcross and her team's hours in the kitchen, soon to be ignored by the two seated royals. Ivy looked at the food in front of her, glancing from dish to dish, platter to platter, tureen to tureen.

"Where is the toast?" she asked, somewhat bemused but retaining her politeness. Before there could be a vocalised reply, three servants had come forward to offer the plate, which lay between the quail's eggs and mackerel pastries.

"Thank you," came her embarrassed reply.

Mother could see the stifling of her daughter day by day, but could not go against the nature of the past, the ceremony of how things had been. The walls flanked with servants for every meal, the constant haranguing and pandering during the day, the handmaids rendering Ivy useless as they undertook every task for her. It had been the same with her. She had tried to lighten the formalities and atmosphere of the castle – simple redecoration, easing of servants' duties, engaging her daughter in more individual activities. Yet still Ivy seemed most at peace on her long walks, often with Laurent.

Laurent.

Despite his unfortunate disposition, his manner was distressing, at best. But his presence made her daughter happy.

Ivy fingered the toast and loosely spread too great a covering of butter before applying old Mr Plant's riccolo jam. She was now used to the ceremonial formation of her life, and to the covering of the table at mealtimes, but she still felt guilt at the amount of food prepared and subsequently wasted. Not that Mrs Maltcross ever seemed to mind. Ivy turned the toast round in her fingers, peering at the pips and lumps in the jam. She became aware that her mother was watching her across the skyline of dish tops, upright spoons and handles. She took a bite of toast.

Seven years had passed since the Queen had discovered her daughter stealing a slice of venison pie from the kitchens, and with the unearthing of other secreted items the truth tumbled tearfully out. Ivy had found a tiny gap in the bordering hedgerow and had been escaping the city.

"Escaping?" her mother had questioned, surprised by the word choice.

"Yes, Mother." A steely look of defiance. "Escaping."

The Queen had tried to forbid her daughter. Ivy rebelled. She had engaged her in countless time-consuming activities. Ivy absconded. She had her followed. Ivy fled. So, in the end she had turned a blind eye in the hope that adventures beyond the boundaries would run their course, seem trivial, and Ivy would embrace the traditions and history of the city. After all, the Queen herself had. Yet, looking at Ivy now, she sensed the girl was a bird not willing to be caged.

Ivy felt her mother's eyes. The guilt of her non-conformity rose in her stomach, flipping the bread, dairy and sugared fruit uncomfortably. It was the look that said, 'I know'. Did her mother understand? Ivy had never crossed the distance between them to ask; the expanse was beset with the obstacles of age and formality. Glancing up, Ivy caught the peculiar look hanging over the littered table, quickly dropping her focus to the plate and stuffing the remaining toast into her mouth. Still chewing, she pushed her chair back.

"With many thanks," she muttered with her mouth full, remembering her training.

"Where are you going?" came the frail voice from the end of the table. Ivy looked up. There was no anger or malice in the tone. Perhaps a hint of longing?

"Umm… to walk the gardens…" Ivy lied, unconvincingly.

A pause.

"Ok," came the uncertain response.

A pause.

"Be careful, darling."

CHAPTER 3

THE GREAT CROSSROADS

Fenwood was a city with an organised structure. Around the outskirts of the dwellings lay the farmed fields where working folk happily toiled the land, making it work for the greater good. Paths and tracks ran between some of these fields that led up to the journey-ways - usable roads that connected Fenwood to the trade routes. Yet these were of little concern to the inhabitants, except for market day. They knew of the roads, they had perhaps even taken a walk to the Great Crossroads to see if it really did exist like was told in the old stories, but these held little interest in their simple, nature-driven lives.

The central housing area was surrounded by the 'Oaken Ring', a ring of great oak trees, which in turn segregated the city from the outer work fields. Within the city, narrow lanes of stone and mud ran between each of the houses, never equally or logistically positioned, merely as if a child had scattered small blocks of wood in a small circular frame. In places the houses were built so close across a path that one could climb from the upper storey of one dwelling into an upstairs window of another (this was often the case in games of 'Hide' and 'Chase' played by the children). The people of Fenwood were vigilant against the threat of fire, which meant that the only real problem of the city was mud during the wet season, when the streets would turn to slush and water. At times like these men would make sled-like vehicles for their families when moving around. Even crime was a non-entity; the city was very small, and everybody was familiar with the other inhabitants – strangers were frowned upon until they could prove their worth. At night, many of the street-crossings were lit, and due to the random street layout there were plenty of these, resulting in few shadows where rogues could lurk.

The labyrinthine formation of lanes around the houses all led into the marketplace, at the centre of which stood the Meeting House. It had initially been voted that every eighth day would be Market Day, when each of the townsfolk could set out a stall, selling crops, meat or some craft that the wives indulged in. Travelling tradesmen often came to sell their goods; extravagant men dealing in luxuries such as fine wines, wooden puzzles or foreign-cultivated pipe tobacco. However, as time progressed, it became commonplace to see stalls in the market place every day, save for the fifth day when the Meeting House and surrounding dirt space doubled as the worship area. The Priest would stand upon the carefully constructed wooden rostrum that jutted out from one of the parallel walls of the Meeting House, preaching across the dusty market area of the glories of Nature. The rest of the days, the large wood-panelled building was used for meetings and the issuing of the daily work rota; the preacher himself spent his time upholding the various rituals that were laid down in books and believed to be important to the day-to-day life of Fenwood.

*　　　　　*　　　　　*

Ivy shut her eyes and took a deep breath, both of the air and of the sense of herself that channelled down through the sun's rays upon her. The colour, lost from her face at breakfast, flooded back. When she opened her eyes again the city below her had also regained colour; the men who had risen to work through necessity now whistled to the beat of their horses' movements and the corn in the fields reached for the sun. Despite visiting other cities, Ivy had never seen another townspeople settlement, but she knew that they would never be this beautiful, not in the days before stone and metal, and even more so now.

Despite the stifling atmosphere of the castle and her frustration at the archaic customs of 'royal life', Ivy felt a deep affection for Fenwood. The walls of her grandiose home crept inwards with each hour that passed when confined within, suffocating her until she could break free and feel the wind in her hair, the grass beneath her feet and life flowing through her veins. Whilst it was her home and she was the successor to the throne, those who upheld Fenwood's rules and traditions frowned upon her going out and exploring. She could not imagine what they were afraid of. Crime was non-existent. Everyone knew her. Perhaps they feared she would not come back… Ivy smiled at this.

A rustle in the trees behind drew her attention and Laurent duly stepped out from the thicket to stand beside Ivy atop the Downs.

"Isn't it beautiful, Laurent," she said, never expecting a reply.

"Without a doubt, my lady. The Gods themselves would find comfort here," came the silken reply. "It is a

shimmering spectacle, as beautiful as it was yesterday."
Laurent looked slyly at her from the corner of his eye,
wondering if she would pick up on his sarcasm.

"No," exclaimed Ivy, unmoving. "It is more beautiful.
And it will be even more beautiful tomorrow."

Their walks together in the fields and woods in and
around Fenwood were well known to its people, but it was
a long time since anybody listened to the rumours of
anything more than companionship between the ill-
matched children. They would walk miles across the open
land, talking and sharing stories. Often Ivy was content to
listen to Laurent's vocal accompaniment on all subjects,
such was his knowledge (much of which was feigned, not
that Ivy knew or would care) and soothing tone, like a soft
cloth on a troubled brow. She did not long for boys and
material possessions, although she could have either at her
call. She was happy, without really knowing what
happiness was.

Laurent waited as she pondered, as was now
customary, but he never had to wait long. And once again
she was off.

"Where will we go today, my lady?" he asked, catching
her up.

"I don't know. We must be home before the cock
crows four and the sun is at its highest, but I wish to go

further than we have before."

"Perhaps beyond the Crossroads?" enquired Laurent.

"You know that Mother has forbidden it," she giggled. "You are meant to be a minder!"

"And not a friend, my lady?"

"Always a friend." Whether they realised it or not, the moment became awkward. Ivy laughed and ran ahead, letting her cotton shirt billow out on the wind. Laurent stared after her.

"Come on, minder!" came the yell from the young lady, as she disappeared like the breeze into the wood. With pain in his heart but laughter in his eyes, Laurent dutifully followed.

Ivy's light footsteps carried her effortlessly through the trees, finding paths and routes across the natural debris. Occasionally she would chase an animal, or stop to run her fingers across the bark of a tree, or, when she remembered, to wait for Laurent. With every step away from the glistening white walls of her chamber she felt the shackles fall, the bonds of tradition hanging ever looser on her, and she longed to go further beyond the boundaries of her limits. Suddenly she realised that the path she was on did lead, eventually, to the Great Crossroads. She had been told many times not to cross onto the Peasant's Way that ran west; it was, supposedly, dangerous as it led through the quarries and unruled lands onto the larger cities. Ivy longed to see them but knew she would be severely reprimanded if discovered, even forced to stay inside, and these moments of freedom were too important to risk.

On the crest of the hill, she could see the black and white painted post that marked the centre point of the crossroads. Ivy halted and looked back. Laurent was bent over, almost crawling on hands and feet up the rise, beastlike, and she could hear him wheezing. It crossed her mind that she was disgusted by him, but the pity for him that overwhelmed her so often flooded back and she called out his name.

"Come on, slowcoach!"

A warped smile touched the corners of his mouth, and he doubled his efforts to reach her; the pain of not being next to her overpowering the anguish of being her companion. Brushing the leaves and dusty mud from his knees and hands, Laurent counted his breaths in and out, in and out, until the hand of the young princess rested reassuringly on his shoulder, and all sense of control vanished. By the time he had built up the courage to put his hand on hers, it had gone.

"Well, we're here," she said in a voice that spoke of her desire to break the rules.

"Tut tut, Ivy, what would your mother say!" Unsure whether he was asking seriously or jokingly, she looked at him, through him, with her piercing green eyes, before stepping forwards onto the crossroads.

It had been called the Great Crossroads for as long as anyone could recall. Fenwood, being the most eastern city, was linked to the other lands by a single road, feeding into the crossroads that sat on the Downs above the settlement. Unlike the remainder of the Fenwood roads, Peasant's Way was embedded with stone, rather than the cobble and mud mix, which meant that it could withstand the heavy-footed traffic of day-to-day supplies, visitors and tradespeople. On market days the traders lined the rough shingle for hours, forming a long, plodding parade before meandering their slow way down the sloping hillsides, passing between the fields and tight-packed houses to the Market Square.

Legend, spoken in Fenwood, told that when the first people arrived at the Lands, they had found a small settlement in the far east already thriving amongst the forest and marshland; thus, 'Fen-Wood' was named. It was a story that people enjoyed telling rather than believed, and the beginnings of the city were long since forgotten. It was generally recognised that it was an ancient, inhabited area with records dating back many, many generations. The

Great Crossroads had been built to link Fenwood to other cities and allow not only trade but also travellers who wanted to experience this strange, quaint city, which still so embraced its natural roots. Whilst visitors dwindled down to none, trade was a necessity and therefore encouraged by both the Queen and those in the nearest cities, even though these were many days and weeks away on horseback.

Ivy stood by the central post, gazing up at the arrows that pointed in each direction to places she had never visited. She had a vague memory of being held aloft by her mother at a very young age to touch the signs, remembering the warmth the Queen had shown her before her life descended into formality and tradition.

"And now that we're here, what next?" teased the servant, limping up beside the girl, dragging his foot slightly behind him. Ivy looked at him with an impish smile.

"Aren't you going to tell me what I'm allowed or not allowed to do?" She looked at him with doe-eyed false sincerity. For a moment he was lost in her gaze. Quickly, Ivy broke the moment.

"A passing trader once told me of a pool nearby, tucked away in a clearing." She glanced around, foolishly wondering if she could see it.

"He was probably just trying to convince you to buy one of those awful jewels you like to hang pointlessly around your neck!" Laurent remarked, aiming for it to sound like a joke, but it came out cloaked in bitterness. "Some sort of magical pool, is it? Do the Gods piss in…"

"Laurent!" Ivy snapped, genuinely disgusted by his attempt at humour. He cowed like a struck puppy. Ivy was angry at her own embarrassment and knew that he was watching her. Again, she looked up at the signpost, looking at the arrows, to where they fruitlessly pointed. Finally, she settled her eyes on the dark mould of the engraved 'Fenwood', and began trudging back along the muddied footpath.

The pool sighed. The trees drooped slightly so that they could trail their age-weary limbs in the cool water. It was not enough that the long months were permeated only briefly by the appearance of the forest child, who wondered at them and bathed in the water that was eager to engulf the youth and keep his young, natural spirit refreshed. The protecting hands of the trees tightened further still around the pool, as if the child somehow warranted a shield.

But with the child once again gone and never any indication of when it would return, the trees resumed days and weeks of emptiness; the time passed taking its toll, the days darkening, the shadows on the pool growing longer.

Where once was great beauty, sickness now endured.

CHAPTER 4

TRADITIONS

Ivy's eyes flickered open at the calling of the cockerel. It was morning. She groaned quietly to herself and pulled her bed covers over her head. The day could wait for her. It had been a humid night and having got up to open her bedroom shutter, she could hear the sounds of Fenwood climbing up the castle walls and creeping into her private world. After the crowing of the cocks, the first workers greeted each other warmly and collected their tools from the store.

"Blessed morning, brother."

"Thank the Gods."

"Fair morning's greetings to you."

"Gods allowing, it will be a fine day," amongst other

niceties.

Then the gentle lowing of the cattle as they were moved from their night barns out into the fields.

Then the trundle of threshing machines.

And the rattle of keys for the first business openings.

Every morning.

You could tell the time of day by it.

Ivy was irrationally irritated by it all.

Her morning musings were interrupted by a sharp knock at the chamber door that conveyed uncertainty rather than annoyance.

"Err… ma'am? No… m'lady?" came the shy voice. Ivy did not respond. Maybe her lady-in-waiting would think she had already got up and gone out.

"M'lady, Ernest told me that you had best be getting yerself up now, m'lady." There was a pause. "It's the corn blessing ceremony today."

"The what?" called out Ivy from her covered realm. Instantly she knew she had given herself away.

"The corn blessing. In the lower fields, right out there beyond the oaken ring. Where they bless the corn." There came another pause. "I put out your dress for the ceremony."

Ivy looked out from her hiding place and scanned the walls of her private chamber, adorned with beautifully colourful, hand-woven tapestries and wall-hangings. Then her eyes fell on the drab, flaxen-dyed smock. She sighed. Then sat upright.

"Freya! Did you hang that up in here during the night?"

Another pause.

"Um. Yes, ma — err, m'lady…"

"Whilst I was asleep?"

"Well… Yes…"

Ivy retreated under her quilted covers and screamed silently to herself.

"M'lady?"

Ivy gritted her teeth.

"Yes. Yes, I'm coming down. Please have some oatmeal ready."

Freya paused again.

"I'm afraid, m'lady, morning mealtime has now ended. You'll need to go right along to the Ritual Hall for practice. To practise. For the corn blessing."

A wooden ornament left Ivy's hand and thudded against the wall, inches from the solid, chamber door.

"Err… m'lady?"

*   *   *

"Then you, Mother, will walk down the middle aisle,

formed by the corn carriers, and approaching the Corn Queen you will curtsy… No, no, not yet, ma'am… Two more steps… Yes, now, nice and low…"

Mr Kitterton danced around and gesticulated wildly as he put the ceremonial party through their paces in readiness for the afternoon's corn blessing. He was a queer fellow; by his lined face you would have guessed him to be somewhere between seventy and death years old, and yet he had the body and exuberance of a man much younger.

"And now your turn, Ivy."

The royal girl was snapped out of her stupor. She was aware of her mother attempting to reproach the Master of Ceremonies.

"Mr Kitterton, you will refer to my daughter as 'm'lady'…"

"With all due respect, Mother, down here you are under my charge." He cast a sideways look at Ivy. "And if she does not buck her ideas up, she shall hear me calling her much worse. Now, shall we go from the beginning again?" He turned and flounced away. Mother stifled a grin and looked over at her daughter to share the joke. But the space by the door that Ivy had absently filled was now empty. The Queen maintained her enigmatic smile, masking her feelings of disappointment and understanding.

*   *   *

Ivy allowed the cool air to fill her lungs, closing her eyes to lose herself in the sensation. She had escaped through the kitchen delivery door, out into the scrubland at the rear of the castle, using a break in the briars that she knew of to half scramble up a track to a knoll. From there she could command a fine view of Fenwood, but still admire many working details from moderate proximity: the smiles of the farmers; the nitter-natter of the weavers, the swaying of the corn. And beyond. Beyond. Out there, past the protective yet restrictive Oaken Ring, she could see vast woodland and wild land and endless possibility. She breathed in the free air. Looking down on the castle, she was sure that little obedient feet would be scampering around cold corridors searching for her; footsteps that echoed in her life, day after day. It was a castle, both beautiful and tiresome, that dominated the skyline and her horizons. Endless parades and ceremonies and dignitaries and traditions. Even her birthday had involved several important customs that had to be upheld, barely allowing for any time to… to what? Be with friends? Her eyes fell at the thought. She knew that so many girls in the city would dream of the luxuries, the dresses, the possessions she had.

She knew that she should be, and was, thankful. Yet she could not shake the feeling that there was much more out there, beyond the Oaken Ring, beyond the castle.

She sensed a dark shadow behind her and, turning, collided with the frail body of Laurent. His hand reached out to her arm to steady himself, or her, or either of them, and remained there.

"Oh! My Princess," – Ivy tutted at the address – "I was going to play a childish trick on you," he croaked. "But it is I who am now startled like an animal!"

"Animals move with far greater ease and grace than you!" she teased with a smile, and he smiled back to hide the sting of her words.

"All animals have their own cunning and clever skills. And their own beauty…"

Ivy sniggered.

"I have beauty," he insisted but his voice had now a hint of defiance and pleading. Ivy smiled again, awkwardly this time, noticing that his withering hand had lain on her arm for too long.

"Laurent, how did you know I was up here?" she asked, frowning, looking away.

"I… I saw you. Saw you going through the gap in the thorny bushes down below," he replied.

Ivy pulled her grey shawl across her shoulders at a chill

that ran through her body.

"May I walk with you?" Laurent asked, trying to be as bright and cheerful as possible. Ivy glanced up into his face and then away. Silently she nodded.

CHAPTER 5

THE VISITOR

Looking back, the people of Fenwood could not pinpoint when he had come. Some thought he had come purely to cause trouble; some believed him to be a mystic from the Outlands; others saw a simple wanderer with kindly eyes and comforting talk.

Hops stood at the bar, cloth in hand, wiping the inside of a washed ale tankard. He eyed the stranger as he shut the inn door against the driving rain behind him.

"Rotten night, friend," said Hops, still somewhat suspiciously, not taking his eyes off the man whilst drying ale pots with a well-worn cloth. At first, he perceived the man as a wanderer or one of the wood folk, but his dress was not that of a man who relied on the land. His clothes may have been sopping wet but they were of expensive velvets and silks. As the man raised his head, Hops saw the man's eyes, a crystal light blue, and smiled – why, he could not say.

"Yes," came the deep voice. "Friend."

"Have you travelled far?" enquired Hops, putting down the now over-dry ale pot.

"I have," replied the man, offering no further explanation. There was a silence, but no awkwardness.

"Would you like a drink? And perhaps some food?" asked Hops, making another attempt to welcome the stranger.

"I certainly would not refuse such hospitality, my friend. Perhaps some milk and a small portion of meat?" The voice was not pleading, but thankful.

"Certainly. I have some fresh game meat, or perhaps some young suckling pig?"

"Suckling pig would be wonderful."

Hops almost bounced to the hatch behind the bar, muttering something inaudible to the shadows within. When he turned, the man was busy scribbling on a scrap of paper. Hops desperately wanted to look at the writing but knew better than to involve himself in the private lives of strangers. He could not help but notice the man's hands, too clean and cared for to have worked manually, and yet he did not seem to have the air of those who worked as aides or clerks. His face was wise and the hair conservative and cared for, his clear pools of eyes seemed a centre of tranquillity. The man looked up, catching Hops' eyes on him. For a split-second Hops saw trouble. The wrinkled brow spread as a smile stretched the stranger's face, and the eloquent voice quashed Hops' fears.

"Forgive me. I, a stranger, come to your inn and do not engage in conversation with my host who has been so kind." He put away his paper and lead, somewhat hurriedly, and crossed his fingers in front of him on the bar. Hops suddenly felt the need to be out of the gaze he now found himself under, and to be using his hands to dry ale pots again rather than shaking in front of him.

"What is your name?" Hops blurted out. The stranger smiled again.

"My name is Rukmahl. I have travelled many moons to see the last remaining natural settlement, to see Fenwood in the valley, and to feel its purity. I have seen wood turn to stone, stone to cold metal, seen warmth grow cold and been sickened by it, until my heart craved once again the virgin settlements of old. My friend, how you must feel to dwell here, where the Gods have chosen to sanctify, blessing the land and its queen with life beyond that of others."

The words flowed like wine into Hops. A cry that seemed so far away alerted him to the readiness of the food and milk. Hops tripped and staggered as he collected it, finally placing the steaming bowl in front of the man. Rukmahl put his nose to the food, smiling at his reflection in the gravy that drizzled over the pig meat.

"My good man," he said upon looking up through the steam, tendrils twirling around his clipped, black moustache. "Never has a stranger been treated more as a king than I have here tonight. Come and join me – bring your finest ale and we shall share stories and warm our hearts on this sombrest of nights."

Before long the two men sat in grandiose chairs by the roaring hearth, sipping Hops' finest ale from the finest flagons. Hops leant in towards the stout man, whom he felt he had known now for many years. He fed off the honey-glazed stories that tumbled eloquently from Rukmahl's mouth, stories of dragons and wars, maidens and murders, gold and pestilence. Somewhere in amongst the tales Hops invited the traveller to stay in his spare room, excusing the excess food and barrels that cluttered the walls. Rukmahl accepted warmly without question.

As with any close community, news of the stranger spread

like the pox.

"Have you heard about the man?"

"He's travelled from far away."

"He's from a different world."

"He heals people with his bare hands."

"He's a dark magician."

"He's of royal blood."

"Those eyes of his glow red."

"Sang very loudly at the 'Givings'."

"Don't go near him, boys; don't go near."

Judgement on the visitor was sorely split, but all were convinced of his mysteriousness.

For the first few days since his arrival the stranger kept a none-too-low profile amongst Fenwood, to the distress and delight of the dwellers whose eyes flittered this way and that to catch a glimpse of the new celebrity. And Rukmahl did not disappoint. Always he appeared in yet more fine cloth of the deepest and richest hues, almost shimmering with silver and golden threads in the light that cut through the buildings. On occasion, a feathered hat might adorn his head, or in his hand he would carry a silver-topped ivory cane. He was all too aware of the effect he had on those who passed him by, and he greeted each and every gaze and glare with an enigmatic smile and a crisp "Good day," coated with velvet. Despite his finely trimmed beard and penetrating eyes, he was not a physically attractive figure; perhaps ungainly at times in his walk, or overly intense in his visage. Yet in that manner, and within those eyes, men sought adventure and women craved his attention.

Wherever he went in those first few days, crowds huddled and cast judgemental eyes over goods he purchased, and even those he fingered and returned to their surface. It became recognised amongst businessmen and traders that the 'gentleman' was, despite the nervousness that descended upon them when he browsed, excellent for business. More stalls than had ever been seen before packed the marketplace on market days after his arrival, whether for his custom or his presence. Men had suddenly found a skill in silverwork or fishing, and the women found good reason to wear their best and brightest garments. Rukmahl (or Mr Rukmahl as some were already calling him) remained gallant, visiting and complimenting every stall, whether for the beauty of the craftsmanship or of the lady turning deep crimson behind it. Once or twice a wry smile wrinkled the leathery face. People assumed it was in joy at their fair and great city; the last remaining natural stronghold that had captured the heart of a wise and noble stranger.

And then he was gone.

Many traders brought out their stall early or dressed it in a new material; businessmen had worked through the night; a gushing aroma of fresh bread and prime produce flooded the streets and huddled on the many corners where the children played stickball. The townsfolk came out under the pretence of browsing and shopping, but whilst hands pointed out their chosen fish, eyes looked back and forth, their minds far from the day's midday meal.

And they waited. But he did not come. Not the next day, or the day after that. Crowds dwindled and the number of stalls depleted. As quickly as he had materialised, Rukmahl had vanished, causing even more of a commotion.

"It was too good to be true."

"I knew it, a scout from the Outlands."

"He's been poisoned."

"Had to go back to his wife."

The men returned to working in the fields, compensating in their longer hours for work that had been neglected in days previous. Summer, the buxom donkey farmer who waved and smiled at the men every morning, once again became the topic of conversation. Certainly, people still spoke of Rukmahl, but another market day came and went with no reappearance, consigning the well-adorned stranger to idle muttering and "Do you remember…" talk. They had really known nothing of him, and he was not of their sort. However, he had affected the life of Fenwood and its people, if even for a short time, and those who tried to deny "such an absurd suggestion" were betrayed by the fidgeting of their eyes and hands. Like the remnants of disease, Rukmahl hung in the air and behind closed doors.

Hops awoke early next market day. After a surprisingly busy previous evening, he had risen to find not only had Farmer Gilletts and Alderhey, the stonemason, broken a table in the midst of their raucous drinking game, but he was completely devoid of suckling pig in the pantry. Taking care not to wake his wife (who really need not know about the pig or table), he pulled on his boots and sauntered into the morning air. Navigating the maze of streets no longer presented the stout man with any need to concentrate and he soon passed underneath the swinging sign for 'Goodlady's Sweet Bites' and into the open square. Several stalls had been erected and their owners were readily arranging produce or craft into an eye-catching display.

"Morning, Hops," came several cries as the innkeeper passed by them into the very centre where Mr Swinton was unpacking boxes of fresh pig meat ready for the day.

"Morning, Swinton," chirped Hops. Swinton glanced up and his eyebrows seemed to smile before his mouth.

"Lovely one, Hops. Summer gave me a huge wave on the way up today so there won't be a cloud in the sky." His bushy moustache bounced as he spoke. "What can I do for you today?"

Hops cast his eye over the meat, noticing the stall that lay next to Swinton's had no cover, goods or owner.

"I'll need... Whose stall is that?" he asked, curiosity getting the better of him.

"No idea," replied Swinton, flattening down his wild hair. "It was here, empty like that, when I turned up."

Hops eyed it with some suspicion.

"Daisy not here, then?" he asked.

"Nope," came the moustached reply. "She's got her prime beef over there today," said Swinton, pointing across the market place, quickly adding, "And the meat from her cows ain't bad either," before descending into bellows of laughter. Perhaps not fully understanding the older man's joke, Hops chose his pig meat and moved away, casting a parting glance at the empty stall as he left, the sound of Swinton's guffaws still resounding around the Market Place.

The glorious weather brought a bustling market day,

the busiest since the stranger, and Swinton lost count of the number of times he had to tell people where Daisy's prime beef was today (although after his first attempt fell on deaf ears he did not repeat the joke). The market was sufficiently animated that most people missed the patter of small feet and streak of small bodies that followed with small hands carrying unmarked, sealed boxes. The boxes were placed neatly in equal rows, stacked on top of one another. Many turned to see the boxes sitting atop the table as if conjured to appear there. Due to the nature of their arrival, there was much angst that overcame any desire to unpack the possible treasures within. Men cast a look and continued past, but several women stopped at the stall, peering at the blank boxes, turning to each other to gabble over what was within and who the owner was.

Then a voice rose above the others. A voice which silenced those who heard it.

"Can I interest you, ladies?" Velvet. Silk. Crimson. Gold.

He had returned.

(iii)

A change in the wind. A new breeze that made the once great trees stand up and take notice. A smell that had not touched them before; sweet, sickly even. And a voice in the air.

The time was coming.

Where was the boy?

CHAPTER 6

THE QUEEN'S FRIEND

The boxes contained small silver vials of various coloured liquids, each with a handwritten label tied on with silken thread. A single word in beautiful script graced the label, along with the colour distinguishing one bottle from the next. On the reverse, the instructions read:

'Add three droplets to a goblet of water and drink without food.'

The potions claimed to be remedies for a multitude of illnesses, ailments and unfortuitous circumstances, from worms to bad breath, syphilis to nightmares. Naturally, Fenwood's three doctors, Boggus, Zaphyr and Grimald, claimed the potions to be nothing more than a floral water mixed with colourant. However, much to their annoyance,

53

none of these renowned men could fully renounce the healing qualities of Rukmahl's natural, bottled remedies. Neither could they stem the tide of townsfolk who turned to the silver vials to cure their back pain, warts, or animal bites. Rukmahl's stall quickly became a focal point three times a week (on the first, third and seventh day) in the Market Square. Traders complained the queue blocked off their stalls, and so moved to other areas of the Square, leaving behind empty plots.

Business grew. Soon Rukmahl's one stall became two, then three and four. The queue grew longer, and whilst Rukmahl had to employ helpers (all of whom were paid handsomely), nearly all sought the foreigner's advice or spoke to him just to hear his golden tongue. It was never made public where the liquids and vials were brought in from, or whether Rukmahl himself wove his magic into creating them, and no one asked, perhaps too afraid of the answer. What did become clear was that Rukmahl's remedies worked (whether physically or psychologically), that his business continued to expand, and that he soon began actively searching for shop space.

*　　　　　　*　　　　　　*

Ivy's hands brushed over the roughness of the leaves and

allowed them to spring back behind her. Laurent stayed several paces back, keeping his eyes on the girl and safe from the sharp slap of the hard, wrinkled branches. Several times he had asked Ivy to slow down, but she pressed on regardless without even glancing back at her appointed friend. In truth, she had forgotten he was with her many times on their walk this day, reminded of his presence only when he caught her up and bestowed more self-confident stories and remarks upon her. Occasionally she found herself wishing that he would stop interrupting the view with his witticisms, but then a joke or quip would catch her smiling before she could allow the thought to manifest. Did she really need a minder anymore? What possible danger could she be in here? In and around Fenwood? She was not sure who it was that asked Laurent to accompany her each day, if anyone. It had never occurred to her that he did it by choice and his own decree… She kept walking.

The colours of sundown painted the white fortress, and as Ivy approached, her shadow clung to the walls in the late afternoon sun. A section of the huge, thickset oaken door swung open as she strolled towards it; her presence at the castle gates having been documented well before she even reached them. As soon as she stepped inside, an old waiting lady handed the princess a warm, damp towelette.

"Now, my dear, do please wipe your hands and face,"

came the cracked, caring voice. "You just don't know what bugs, beasties and bacteria pollute the air out there, and now it could be all over that pretty face of your'n."

Ivy turned to reproach the lady, but could not stop the warm grin that spread across her face.

"Mrs Rochester, please tell me you haven't been waiting here all afternoon?!"

"Of course not, sweetheart," chuckled the portly lady, shaking her head so that the tightly pulled bun in her hair moved from side to side. "I've made your bed, sorted your wardrobe into the ceremonial clothes you'll need this week, dusted your bed chamber and woven the repairs to the tapestry in your study – it's been a rather full day m'lady!"

There was not even a hint of remorse in the doughy face. Ivy, in return, shook her head, still smiling warmly, appreciatively.

"But what have you done for yourself? When do you ever see Mr Rochester?"

"Mr Rochester?!" bellowed the lady-in-waiting. "Do you think I have time for a useless man in my life, getting under my feet all day?!" And both ladies, young and old, laughed. "You take my advice, my love, steer clear of men; nothing but trouble they are!"

Ivy took the generous arm in hers and together they

walked into the castle grounds; Ivy finally slowing her pace and her lady-in-waiting waddling along at her side.

Laurent slunk from the shadows of the arch of the front gate, long forgotten about. Looking down, he picked out Ivy's light footprints in the mud and followed the trail, carefully placing his feet into the imprint of hers. Yet, after six steps he stopped. It was obvious that his feet were bigger, and those delicate prints were undeniably crushed beneath his. He stepped to the side and bending down, he traced the outline of the next footprint with his finger. It was perfect.

A minute passed before he realised that several eyes of castle hands were on him. He stood, awkwardly. He tried to smile, but what happened to his mouth and face was grotesque and somehow wrong. Even the "good afternoon" stuck in his throat with choked back tears. Dropping his head once again into his stoop, Laurent lumbered across the courtyard and dissolved into the darkness of the corridors.

*   *   *

The look on his face seemed nothing short of nonchalant – a relaxed brow, half smile, and even short sighs at the amount of time this was taking. Yet inside, Rukmahl was carefully calculating every estimate and measurement that his workers were throwing at him. They scurried this way and that, measuring walls, windows, selling spaces, whether the drapes would hang to the correct distance from the floor; generally turning Mr Mallory in circles. His tobacconist shop had long since dwindled in profit due to the success of homegrown pipe weed. Nevertheless, it was one of the original shops in Fenwood, traditionally standing on Market Corner. Parents had, for generations, told their young to meet under the pipe sign hanging from Mallory's Tobacco if they got lost in the crowd. Mallory was not selling his shop, but he could do nothing to stop Rukmahl and his whirlwind from entering and calculating. After all, he was a respectable man, who no doubt intended to purchase some of Mallory's finest tobacco, cigarillos, or cigars. Indeed, the heavyset man, draped today in a purple cloak, now stood twirling a rich, cedarwood and dewberry fern cigar in his fingers. In any normal hand the cigar appeared a monster of carefully rolled tanned paper, but in Rukmahl's hands it looked none too dissimilar from the five sausages that were attached to each palm.

The two piercing eyes gazed out through the glass screen across the bustling square. Many people continued to pass by Mallory's to catch a glimpse of what was going on, but seeing pools of blue staring back at them, they hurried on, not wanting to be recognised. Rukmahl ceased rolling the cigar in his fingers, and as if they had noticed this tiny sign, the workers stopped. Rukmahl did not turn to face Mallory.

"My friend," he growled, raising the cigar to his nose. "This cigar smells divine. You must have had help from the Gods to create such staggering aroma." And at this, he turned. Mallory played with his waistcoat pockets as he fell under the gaze.

"I have always tried to lead an honest life, in order to please those on high," he said, sounding much more confident than he felt. Rukmahl smiled.

"Yes; the Gods look favourably on folk like you, and it is well-deserved, my good man." He crossed to Mallory. "I, on the other hand, like to trust to my own hard work and, let's say, skill to achieve my goals." He reached past Mallory, bringing his bulk very close to the tobacconist's slender frame, and took a box of cedarwood cigars from the counter.

"I would like to purchase a box of these wonderful cigars, Mr Mallory."

"Of course," Mallory said through a forced smile. "Is that all?"

"Oh no," said Rukmahl, unblinking. "Tell me, friend,

do you hand engrave cigar cutters?"

"Certainly, sir—"

"Good," interjected Rukmahl. "Give me your finest cigar cutter with the letter 'R' in your most elegant and expensive script."

"Very good, sir. Anything else?"

"Your shop."

*   *   *

The Queen coughed. Not a polite cough into a silken handkerchief that one expects of a divine ruler, but a deep, hacking cough of a pipe-smoking drunk. It took her some moments to recover.

"Ma'am?" uttered the servant, bending down to catch a look at the crumpled lady's face. "Are you unwell?"

The Queen composed herself and stood up to her full (if somewhat diminished by age) height.

"I'm fine thank you, Ernest." She smiled, finally drawing out her handkerchief to mop the beads of sweat that were hanging beneath the fine, silver fringe. She reached out and touched the butler's elbow. "You know as well as I do, Ernest, that people our age must take care of themselves in inclement weather." She made her way back to her wardrobe. The man shifted his grey-haired head in the direction of the window, looking at the sun with some confusion.

"Yes," he muttered, half to himself. "Of course." He cleared his throat and addressed the lady again. "Will that be all, Mother?"

She giggled at the use of the term.

"Yes, thank you, Ernest," she said, turning to give him a beaming smile. He did not return the smile and made for the door. In turn her lips dropped the moment his back was to her, but as he made to leave, she called after him.

"Ernest!"

He looked to her again, this time both their faces were solemn. "I am fine," she said. He simply nodded and shut the door behind him.

The Queen sank into the cushioned seat that matched the ornate dressing table, carved for her by the royal carpenters. Yet her eyes fell not onto the realism of the ivy leaves depicted in the childish innocence of the cherubs in the woodwork, but at the frail, withering old lady who looked back from the mirror. The mass of creams and powders that covered the dressing table surface had done wonders to hide the truth from the people of her fair realm, but perhaps mostly from herself: she was old, and she would die. The birth of Ivy at such a late stage in her life had demonstrated her youth and vigour to her people, who were unaware that in the weeks that followed the miraculous birth, she had struggled to hold onto her own life. Yet survive she did, and even though she never regained her full strength, some of the focus had moved onto her beloved daughter allowing the Queen to take less of the limelight. Now Ivy was sixteen, beautiful and loved by the people; Fenwood would be ready for her to rule when Mother passed on.

The Queen coughed again. She rested her hand on her chest as the wheezing subsided. Her left hand raised the embroidered lace handkerchief to her mouth, and she spat out the phlegm. Nervously, she crumpled it up in her aching hand and threw the cloth into the fire, not ready to check the spittle in its midst. Waiting a moment, she breathed easier before reaching up and unclasping the choker from around her neck. The sense of freedom shocked her, and she could feel without even touching it how swollen her throat must be. Looking once again into the mirror she sighed and allowed her thin, veined hands to open one of the drawers to the side. She removed a beautiful, fragranced set of writing paper and a quill, plumed with a magnificent blend of red and blue feathers. The cream paper was laid out carefully in front of her at an angle for writing. She dipped the quill tip into a pot of ink. For a final time she looked at the vaguely recognisable figure in the mirror, and began to write:

Dear Mr Rukmahl…

          *   *   *

The door slammed, rattling the windowpanes and much of the stock, but Mallory breathed a sigh of relief. He had withstood the repugnant man's displays of power - both his money and will. It ultimately stood that he, Mallory, had nothing but the shop to pass to his son and nothing – no money in the world – would rob his boy of his inheritance. Mallory had smelt the pork crackling and expensive wine on Rukmahl's breath, so close was his face, before the intimidating walrus had growled in rage and stormed out, leaving the shop interior shaking and the exterior sign swinging wildly.

Out in the street, Rukmahl tried his utmost to keep his anger from boiling over. A crowd had gathered around him like gawpers at a murder scene, asking many variations of the same questions. Rukmahl silenced them with the waving of his hands.

"I am touched that you are so concerned as to my business transactions" – there came a general hubbub from the crowd – "I have spoken at great length with the good Mr Mallory about shop prices in general. The man is important to this city and I was never enquiring as to his shop" – more hubbub interrupted him – "I am only too aware of the generational family orientation of the business, and I have nothing but respect for the Mallorys' business. As a long-standing and well-respected man in this community, I merely sought his advice in purchasing." The crowd grew quieter, unsure of the look that seemed to pass over the worldly face, making him somewhat wild rather than resplendent. "Needless to say, his advice, as always, was most considered and I continue to look for shop space. However, my friends, until that time the Market Square shall be home to my small business venture, and I look forward to seeing you all there very soon!"

The crowd broke into applause, soon forgetting their insecurities, and when Rukmahl's workers dispersed towards the stalls, they followed, leaving the proprietor alone in the dust. He licked his lips and looked skywards at the pipe sign. Reaching up with his ivory-topped cane, he stopped it swaying in the breeze. His gaze remained there, fixed. Suddenly, violently, the solid cane-top came crashing through the sign, splitting and splintering the stained wood. With renewed purpose he tucked the cane under his arm and inconspicuously (for once), left the Market Square.

*   *   *

Mother laid the pen quill to rest in the designated glass pot so as not to stain the woodwork of the dresser. She picked up a small golden bell and rung; the sound of a hundred nightingales flooded the room and washed along the corridors through the great white castle. The letter was now finished and, as the ink dried, she read aloud:

Dear Mr Rukmahl,

I am aware that you have become a figure of some repute within our fair city in a short period of time. There is talk of your wisdom and kindness, as well as your brilliance with remedies.

I would have you keep this information, as well as this letter, safe and secret. I have fallen ill – not seriously, but enough that I begin to contemplate that I must plan for my daughter's future.

I require not only a man of medicine but a man of honest words who, unlike my doctors, will give me impartial advice and not just words I want to hear. I trust the people of my city and they speak most highly of you. Therefore, I request a meeting with yourself – a private consultation – at which I can meet the newest and most respected member of Fenwood, and judge for myself if you are indeed as wise and worldly as reports suggest. Mr Rukmahl, in truth, I need a friend not an advisor.

In two days' time, at the fall of the sun, you will be sent for.

M

She hoped that it did not appear desperate or pleading, but remained authoritative as well as caring. She did so need a new voice, one which would not whimper and pander to her needs, but tell her truthfully what could be done for the good of the city, and her daughter. A new opinion. An outsider's opinion. If she met the man but once, at least it would provide her with something other than her usual routine. So many people had told her how wonderful the man was – could they all be wrong?

The creak at the opening of the door startled her, and she jumped to face the kindly silver-haired man.

"Ernest, I have a letter for you to deliver. Make sure you take it yourself, and directly, to the man with the medicine stall."

Ernest raised his eyebrows.

"M'lady, is this wise? A royal visit so soon after his arrival? He is not royalty himself."

"Ernest, reports reach me that he has great wisdom, and I wish to meet him." Her harsh tone softened. "Besides, we can make it far less posh and stuffy – you can be there." She giggled, and Ernest's concerned face broke into a smile.

"Thank you, Ernest," she said warmly. "You are a true friend." He nodded. "Oh, and Ernest? Let's not tell Ivy about the coughing." The elderly man looked puzzled.

"Will she not notice, ma'am?"

"Ernest," the Queen looked at him with honesty, "she would need to be here to notice…"

CHAPTER 7

SICKNESS AND HEALTH

Many mouths whispered the hushed secret that the entire castle now knew: he was coming.

Hops ran his cloth proudly over the shining wooden table, still smiling at the compliments that the Summerton family had given today's mutton. The numbers at the tables were dwindling after the evening meal rush; those left were sipping ale and nibbling at leftovers, blowing out their cheeks and leaning back in contentment. He became aware of two men talking about Mr Rukmahl to his left, and he allowed his ears to tune in to their conversation (something he did not often do – he respected the privacy of his guests). He had always felt honoured that the broad, successful man had appeared first at his establishment. He knew that it had boosted his business and would regale customers with the story, when requested.

"…Look, it ain't no secret that Mother ain't so good these times," said one of the men, a bearded worker with black under his nails.

"I knows it," came the reply of his younger friend, "and she's called in his help. Reckon he must have some potion or summat to help her, Gods willing."

Hops moved across to the men.

"Gentlemen," he interrupted, apologetically, "but what is that you say?"

The bearded man was only too happy to pass on his news.

"The merchant, the chap with all the bottles and things. He's been called to the castle, he has."

"The Queen, Mother, can't be well," butted in the other man, to the annoyance of his older companion.

"Aye," he continued, "ain't that something."

Hops nodded, smiled, and left the men to continue their conversation. As he let the door to the kitchen close behind him, he wondered why he felt a slight anxious knot in his stomach.

*   *   *

It had been two days since the letter had been delivered amid raised eyebrows and nods across crowded rooms. Mother remained somewhat oblivious to the furore she had created, and Ivy had not been told at all. A silent decree had been passed by those in service that this was not something to worry the young princess with. Besides, she would find out when he arrived. Why they were reluctant to let Ivy meet the exotic businessman, no one could quite explain, but the general unease that still surrounded the outsider after many months of residing in Fenwood meant that, despite his impressive success with medicines, advice and flattery, he was still just that: an outsider.

The order filtered down that no such dinner or formal welcome was to be extended to Mr Rukmahl; he would visit, briefly, and then be on his way. Mrs Maltcross quickly tore up her proposed menu at the news. Mr Simmons sighed with relief at not having to reshape the topiary hedges. But the Queen remained uncharacteristically distant from the people who loved to serve her. She took to having meals sent up to her room and delegating the overseeing of rituals. She passed this off to those who did speak to her as fatigue, but in truth she began to contemplate her place on high with the Gods. It would take many years to educate Ivy in the traditions of

Fenwood. In fact, the girl displayed no interest in the formalities and, watching her daughter running free without a care in the world, Mother had not the heart to burden her child. Yet, Ivy had to know. The ageing beauty of the Queen once again looked back from the mirror and a sad smile of inevitability crept across her lips, creases forming heavily at the corners. Pulling her soft white hair back from her forehead, some of the lines on her temple disappeared in the tightness of the grip. The smile broadened; There's life there yet, she thought to herself, there's still time.

Ernest almost ignored the sound of the bell, such was the result of not being summoned for two days. He hastily buttoned the top of his linen tunic and cursed his two-day stubble as he half-trotted along the well-trodden path to the Queen's chamber. The sound of his aged knuckles on the chamber door resounded down the corridor; Ernest wondered what the rapping sounded like inside the room. Quickly, he checked over his uniform and sighed again at the roughness of his cheeks. But still there came no reply at the door. He knocked again, this time adding a call of "Ma'am?" It was only a moment before the reply came, soft and welcoming.

"Yes, Ernest, come."

The room was immaculate, more so than usual,

although nobody had been in to clean. On the dressing table stood the various tubs and bottles that had, until this moment, been kept from view. As was his custom, Ernest entered and quietly closed the door behind him. The door gave its click into place (a familiarity that Ernest smiled at), and as he turned to the room his gaze fell not onto his mistress but a tapestry of ancient ritual in gaudy golds and crimsons and rustica. He surveyed the less adorned areas of the rose room, half expecting the Queen to be cowering after two days of solitude.

"Ernest," said a soft voice, diverting his attention to the far side of the bed. Through the netted veil of the bed curtains he could see the lady, dressed in her finest garb, almost shimmering in the late afternoon light; a reincarnation of the ever-youthful maiden that Fenwood loved, causing Ernest to inadvertently drop his jaw and breathe in sharply. The majestic figure glided along the side of the bed, running an outstretched hand across the white silken mesh fabric until it found the finely carved corner post, where a finger embraced the oaken carving. Ernest's brow furrowed as he looked at the creased skin on the fingers. The Queen stepped past the canopy into the servant's full view; his gaze frozen. The face that he had seen so youthful not moments earlier seemed now pulled and wrinkled, harbouring dark crevices and congealed facial paint. The glide had become a stumbling shuffle, as if Father Time was pushing hastily at her back.

"Mother, I have—"

The Queen silenced him with a raised hand.

"Please, Ernest – don't." Their eyes held with an understanding of age and ceremony. "Just fetch him. And be discreet."

*   *   *

The messenger boy squeezed and ducked his way through the maze of limbs and baskets, seeking the centre of the market. From behind his stall, Rukmahl followed the trail of cries, from a simple, "Oh!" to "Mind where you're going!" and with a couple of cries of "Thief!" thrown in. He sensed a message was on its way to him and sought the carrier with a weighty urgency. Yet, when the boy reached the stall he was greeted by the dwarfish helpers, with the prestigious owner sitting behind, scanning his nails with a sense of nonchalant indignancy.

"Sir!" yelped the scruffy haired boy. Rukmahl looked down his nose and replied with a grunt rather than a verbal retort. "Letter for you, sir." Nothing could hide the speed at which the letter transferred from the child's hand to the greedy recipient's. Hungry eyes scanned at first the elegant scrawl, only taking in the point and not admiring the structure or scripture (as was customary). After the third scan he became aware that the boy remained quiet, still, and open-palmed. The overweight, gaudy man smiled awkwardly at the boy and reached into a canvas bag down by his left suede boot. The boy attempted to contain his glee, knees shaking in anticipation. A cold disc was pressed into the clammy palm and short, grubby digits closed around it. He set off back through the crowds, pushing aside tunics and dodging flailing elbows, to find a safe spot to survey his treasure. There, beneath the window box of Blatt's parchment shop, he uncurled his fingers. The disc shone, silver, as it should. But it was no coin. In his hand lay a now mud-stained tin lid, the label across which read 'Odour Repellent'.

*   *   *

Collectively, the castle held its breath. Nobody knew exactly why the man had been sent for, but, regardless of his reputation, it was uncommon for people to enter the castle.

Despite the Queen's insistence that he would not be fed, Mrs Maltcross had thrown together several dishes. Messengers had been sent into the town, independent of the Queen, to find out the man's favourite fare. The extent of the response had been alarming, both in terms of quantity and extravagance, so the talented cook had settled for those she felt confident of impressing with. She need not have bothered.

The guards at the wall gates watched Rukmahl's bulk trudge up the hill on the well-trodden path leading to the castle. For a man sent for instantly he seemed to be taking his time, but as he neared them the two young men could see the red cheeks and perspiration that revealed immense effort.

"The Queen's carriages must all be in use then, gentlemen?" he said when he reached the guards, laughing heartily. Yet, as the tunicked men joined him in jest, they detected annoyance and even repulse in the seemingly tranquil eyes. Nevertheless, their doubts were soon forgotten as they lost themselves in Rukmahl's verbose flattery and engaging conversation. The talk had given the portly man enough time to catch his breath and restore the healthy tan glow to his face. He interrupted the younger man's flow (blabbering about his wife's craft or some such nonsense) and remarked crisply, "Gentlemen I feel we could bring sunshine to the valley with your conversation, but the Queen awaits."

"Oh dear, of course," stammered the interrupted

guard, remembering his duty. Together the men pushed on the heavy oaken doors, and they creaked inward. Rukmahl smiled, unseen by the guards, a smile that seemed somehow out of place.

"Thank you," he said, and walked through the gateway with his chest pushed out and head held high. The doors closed with a weighty clunk behind him.

Ivy's room was on the second level of the castle, giving her a direct entrance onto the interior 'battlement', which served more as a balcony from where she could overlook the plentiful and carefully structured garden, than a fortification. This decision had been taken so that she could gaze out over the beauty of the castle (her mother looked out over the realm) and be thankful for it. Few suspected that she ever dreamt of the world outside and grew ever-weary of regimental allurement. As she ran a brush through her brown hair she looked not into the mirror, but rather through it. The clunk of the gate drew her eyes from behind the reflection and, without stopping the fluid brushing motion, she glanced sideways through the stone opening. She recognised the broad man waddling along the pathway and chuckled to herself as the only observer of his faltering at the shrubbery at the cross paths. Ivy was aware that the grandly-garbed man was new to the town, and of some repute, but her growing distance, both literally and metaphorically, meant she knew not his business, his name or why he would be meandering his way through the garden. For a moment she questioned how she had allowed such a divide to creep between herself and the life of Fenwood – until the realisation fell that, whether rightly or wrongly, it did not bother her.

*   *   *

Rukmahl swore under his breath as he met yet another cross path. He had successfully mastered the labyrinth of streets that was Fenwood so quickly and yet the royal garden, despite being only waist height, was proving something of a maze. A fantasy of flattening the whole blasted plot flashed before his eyes. What a waste of space. He reached out a chunky hand to a rose head that dared to jut out into his path, closing finger and thumb around its neck and snapping it like the wing off a fly. The sensation gave him some pleasure, until the realisation that someone could be watching; he carefully slipped the rose head into a buttonhole in his moleskin, three-quarter length, crimson, silk-lined coat, and guessed left at the junction.

*   *   *

Ernest had escorted the Queen from her chamber to one of the day rooms; he had not had to guide her or take her arm, but he had walked alongside her as a companion, keeping a secretly watchful eye lest she stumbled, which she did not. The Queen settled herself into a lounge chair, a resplendent silver and mauve floral design that provided one of many bursts of colour in the mahogany panelled room. Other pieces of furniture held aspects of silvers and purples, from carved and coloured wooden pieces to deep tapestries or gilded lining. The only colours at odds came from a large painting above the fireplace showing the Queen peering out from behind jet black hair which itself stood out from a ruffled green dress, low at the shoulders. The background depicted a forest scene and a plaque at the bottom, within the frame, simply read 'Mother'. Gazing at herself, the Queen suddenly regretted agreeing to the meeting being held in this room. A set of glasses and a decanter sat on the oval table in front of her, behind which sat an empty, formal chair.

"Will you require any wine, ma'am?" Ernest asked from his place by the door.

"Just water, thank you, Ernest," answered the Queen. Ernest nodded and turned to leave. "Oh, and Ernest?" He turned back to face his mistress. "Please remind Mrs Maltcross that we will not be needing any food."

*   *   *

Rukmahl's demeanour changed many times as he was taken on various stages of his journey through the somewhat time-tainted castle. He had been official but polite with the guards at the front door; charm and swagger had drizzled from him as the servant girls accompanied him to the Master of Ceremonies. The traditionalist administrator had been won over by the man's flattery of the 'old ways'. Finally a shining coin in the palm of an aspiring servant, given the job of escorting Rukmahl to the day room, had enabled him to learn all he needed to know to equip himself for the Queen.

The door to the day room was handcrafted in oak, panelled and carved, a gateway to those granted to access to the Queen. The burly visitor's eyes widened in delight at his destination, but he checked his reaction as an armoured man, tall, athletic and powerful in build, stepped from a small chamber to the side.

"Good day," uttered the man in a measured tone. He rested his hand on the sword strapped to his side.

"My good man," oozed Rukmahl's response, "what an incredible honour it is to be granted such a unique opportunity, and I thank you graciously Mr…?"

There was no change of expression or false nicety from the official.

"Tindal. Chief Tindal," came the curt reply.

"Well, Chief Tindal," continued Rukmahl, "I do hope…"

"Knock and wait," interrupted the guard before nodding and departing, leaving the large man, bedecked in finest, gaudy cloth, alone and smarting at the interruption.

*   *   *

"What? No food at all?" Mrs Maltcross gawped. The slight shock and sharpness in her voice, though subtle, was enough to halt the entire kitchen. Ernest faltered.

"Err, no… as is Mother's request."

Mrs Maltcross pursed her already wafer-thin lips, gulped and gave a solitary nod.

"As she wishes." She turned away, annoyed not with her queen, but at Ernest's sudden need to apologise as an entire kitchen glared at him, hands full of knives, batons and formidable looking lumps of dough.

*   *   *

Large knuckles rapped on the thick, panelled door. There

was no instant reply, and so Rukmahl engulfed the crafted handle in his grip and slowly opened the door.

"You may come in, sir," came the voice from the room. Rukmahl stepped inside. He made sure not to react to any of the surroundings, despite being impressed, and focused his attention on the lady who remained seated in front of him. Her emerald dress was clearly of fine cloth, and she kept her hands folded under an animal hide throw on her lap.

"Your Majesty," he said warmly, with a smile that rearranged his fleshy face. He stood next to the empty chair; he knew that ceremony would be expected.

"Please, sit," she said, without returning the smile. Rukmahl folded the length of his jacket behind him and did his best to place himself gracefully into the seat. Once settled he looked up again, meeting the eyes that studied him from across the table. "Water?" she asked flatly. He desperately wanted to say yes, but declined with a polite half raising of the hand. For a moment they sat looking at each other, as if contemplating the opening move of some strategic game.

"Sir," said the Queen, sighing and dropping her shoulders. "It is not the custom to invite townsfolk into the castle."

"Then I am honoured, ma'am," Rukmahl interjected

with sickliness. The Queen kept her gaze on him.

"Sir, you do not need to use your buttery compliments to try and win favour – I have met enough ambassadors to see through such duplicity. What I need from you, sir, is honesty, loyalty and confidentiality." Rukmahl's face registered enough gravitas for her to continue. "I understand, sir, that you hold a wealth of knowledge in the field of ailments and medicines, somewhat alternative in nature, that have helped you rise to some authority in my city."

Rukmahl suppressed a smile. "It is an area I have long studied, ma'am – you are well-informed."

Finally, the Queen broke the gaze and her eyes fell, looking far beyond the man in front of her. There was a pause.

"I am dying."

She did not look up to see his reaction, but suddenly the man in front of her seemed bigger in his chair. With an audible hint of defeat in her voice, she continued. "I am old, and I know my time has come, but I must remain alive until my daughter is ready and prepared to rule. The royal physician is a kindly man but speaks in coated answers and detours. I am prepared to try new remedies, but I must know the truth." Here she looked up again at the man who filled the chair opposite, whose stare now seemed to diminish her. "Can you help me Mr Rukmahl?"

For a moment she felt entirely vulnerable before him and as he leant forward towards her, she wondered if his hands could crush her. But they took hold of her shaking, aching fingers so tenderly, calmly, and the understanding that flooded from his eyes soothed her panic.

"My queen," his voice seemed to sing, "I am at your service."

*   *   *

Rukmahl became a common sight at the castle over the coming weeks, splitting opinion amongst all clerks, workers and servants as he had done in the city. The Queen grew no better under his remedies, but neither did she grow worse. Packages would arrive scrawled with his cumbersome hand, purporting to contain ingredients that baffled the royal physician; the Queen devoured them all, and became evermore reliant on his remedies, his truth and his company. Rukmahl, in turn, grew increasingly arrogant and powerful and gluttonous, even selling his goods now emblazoned with the royal emblem. The words which had poured like wine upon his arrival were now reserved for those with titles or money or influence (although he was occasionally spotted also with known hoodlums). He was seldom seen at his multitude of stalls, and it was rumoured that his money and influence infiltrated many businesses and clerical organisations, as well as his noted influence over the Queen. She began to take his advice on matters of city life and clerical business, drinking in his words and concoctions without question, ignoring the warnings from her usual trusted advisors and rumours which reached her ears.

The ever-loyal Tindal kept a watch on Rukmahl's movements. He mainly detested the flamboyant slug and had done so since their first encounter. Yet he could not deny Rukmahl's good deeds for the people of Fenwood whatever his true intention. Rukmahl could not hide his daily activities, announcing himself with both sheer size and volume. Tindal, however, had no access to him in the Queen's or his own chambers and, despite his service to the townsfolk, the guard feared this was where he was creating his mischief and slow destruction. For the first time in his life Tindal felt powerless and he sensed Rukmahl knew it. The Queen had subconsciously allowed Rukmahl's imperious nature unaware of how vulnerable it made her. Tindal felt it his duty to catch Rukmahl in the act of treason (as he suspected) but the new 'favourite' was too clever. He had deceived the people of Fenwood with his feigned good will. Most dangerously, he had deceived the Queen.

*   *   *

In the late season, as the weather wettened and cold bore down on the natural settlement, Mallory passed away. His passing was sudden but not accounted for as suspicious. Even Tindal had no cause to question the manner of his death. What raised many questions, behind closed doors, was that the shop was not left to his only son. Thirteen days after the tobacconist was closed, the shop space reopened, as a medicine store, bearing Rukmahl's name and the royal emblem. A will was provided confirming that Rukmahl had inherited the store after a 'long and treasured friendship', which went uncontested by the young Mallory (who went on to lose large sums of money in gambling games). What was clear was that Rukmahl provided the good people of Fenwood with advice and tonics, and flooded the darker recesses of the city with his opinions and potions. The Queen was the beloved figurehead of the city, but her power was faltering, flaking away with the withering of her skin and drowning in the elixirs she now wantonly poured down her swollen gullet. Rukmahl held her frail frame in his engorged hands; a 'sickness' in the heart of Fenwood. Only the very wise appreciated the irony that such a 'sickness' dealt in health, but no one had the courage to speak against him.

And to all this Ivy remained oblivious.

CHAPTER 8

IVY AND THE BOY

Ivy sat atop the Downs, eyes in the direction of the Market Square far below, but not seeing the people who milled around. Her look had a more distant longing, swimming in the dreams her vision fixed upon. She had left without Laurent; the closeness of their relationship strained by Ivy's desire to be left alone, and a growing awareness of his gaze upon her. She loved Fenwood, her mother, the people, Laurent; yet her dreams took her beyond stifling tradition and ever-watchful eyes. She pulled her knees up to her chin and rested there, hugging them closer with her arms. The late afternoon sun lay on a pillow of cloud, casting beautiful oranges, pinks and blues across the valley. The trees on the opposite side of the valley were silhouetted, as the mist began to descend and the temperature to drop. Ivy pulled her shawl tighter around her shoulders but could not contain the shiver that travelled through her body. It was clearly time to go. Her absence would have, without doubt, been noted; but there was something in the stillness of the day and sheer wonder of the colours on the skyline that kept her there, despite the impending cold.

A slight rustle in the bushes to her left drew her gaze from the valley and she craned her neck to catch a glimpse of the mouse or creature that had disturbed her from her daydream. Seeing nothing, she picked herself up from the ground and brushed her feminine hands over the soft fabric of her dress, knowing the lecture she would get if she returned to the castle with stains and natural debris attached to the fine clothing.

There it was again, the briefest of sounds in the brush; a twig breaking or leaves being brushed aside. Ivy moved closer to find out what creature was taking such an interest in her.

"Hello?" she beckoned in a childish voice. "Come out. Don't be scared."

She pushed back the branches closest to the ground, but no animal scurried away. Slightly disappointed but not surprised, the princess carefully allowed the small branches to fall back into place, making sure not to break anything. As she did, an imprint on the ground became apparent. Bending closer, she traced the outline with her finger – a curve, almost a semi-circle, that branched out on both sides. What small creature was heavy enough to make such a shape in the ground? Ivy chuckled to herself at the thought of a hugely obese mouse squatting in the undergrowth and rolling away as she rummaged after him and… She gasped and pulled away her blackened finger, as if she'd been stung. The imprint was a human foot. She gasped again. Somebody had been watching her. Ivy stood up quickly, surveying the land around her. There were not too many bushes; they can't have gone far.

"Hey!" she cried. "Who's there?"

The cry clearly startled the voyeur and a patch of scrubland to her right shook as the watcher took to its heels. Ivy ran as fast as her cotton dress and silken undergarments would allow. As she reached the gorse bushes and nettles, her slippers lost their footing on the dampening grass. One leg twisted beneath her and her right followed, sliding to the ground, striking her thigh on a jutting rock. Grimacing with the pain, her wet-eyed squint was drawn by the movement of a figure. She had been right; it was a human, but as they disappeared down the track there was something incredibly animalistic in the greenish-brown colour of their skin and the scampering on all fours. They were so sleek and majestic, almost beautiful to behold. Ivy longed to see them, so far beyond the realm of her sheltered existence. Despite the dirtying of her dress and a stinging pain in her right thigh, she pulled herself to her feet, not even brushing off the dust and grass, and trotted in the direction the wild person had galloped.

The path led downhill through a tunnel of trees, and as it curved around a corner, she once again spotted the creature – unmistakably, this time, a boy. Squatting on his haunches, supported by his fists on the ground in front of him, head cocked to his shoulder, observing. Ivy slowed her pace. As she walked stealthily forward, the forest child bent lower. Despite his rugged and forest-worn appearance, he was perhaps a similar age to her. When she was only a hundred paces away, he turned and bounded off. Ivy set off again in pursuit, but clearly not able to keep pace. After an initial clearing the path led off through the trees, meandering between bark pillars, cutting between nettles and wildflowers. It dawned on Ivy that she had never been this far from home before, that she was breaking her boundaries, and that, ultimately, she was lost. Yet her desire to see the boy again pushed her on along the debris path, slowing only to see the bursts of colour; red, purple and yellow through the green. The trees began to close in on both sides and the girl ducked under a shield of low-hanging, leafed branches, almost like a curtain, and stood up in the clearing beyond.

It was a pool. So clear, so still, so silent. Ivy was startled by the sight of such tranquility and magic, kept from view by impressive guardians of ash, elm and oak, and other trees that she could not name. She stepped lightly forward, as though invading somebody's secret. The pool was not round but elongated, curving to the left behind overhanging branches. A path ran to the right, hugging the bank; clearly there had once been a matching one on the left side, but this had been taken by a purple-berried bush that Ivy had never seen before. On the surface of the pool lilies drifted happily, greeting each other with a fleeting touch before dancing through the reeds and rushes. Ivy lost her breath. The wind began to form a soft symphony around her. She listened and watched the lilies dance in time, as the great arms of the trees conducted the performance. The water looked so clear and calm that Ivy had to stop herself from jumping in. Instead, she stooped at the near side, running her fingers over the soft surface of the pool. Immersing her hands, she washed them before bringing the pure liquid to her face, refreshing her like she had never known at the stone basins at home.

Suddenly she remembered why she had stumbled upon

this glorious place and stood, searching for the boy. She moved along the bank, keeping to the path, peering through the trees. He was only half hiding from her. Across the back of the pool, a crude bridge had been made some time ago. Signs of age adorned the rail and walkway, like decoration from its still standing kin. There in the centre of the bridge he squatted, gazing over the rail at her. She stopped. This time she did not move towards him, but waited. Neither breaking eye contact, hers gentle and welcoming, his unblinking. Carefully he put his hands to the ground and, as before, moved like an animal around the bank.

The pool waited. The wild boy kept watching and picking his way with caution, but great poise. Ivy's eyes never left his. When he was only fifty paces away, she crouched to his level, and he drew so close that Ivy could feel the warmth of his breath on her face. She remained still. Once, twice, he sniffed the air around her. His hands felt rough as he touched the smooth skin on her arm, and then her face. He let her hair run through his fingers and a twitch of a smile flashed at the corners of his mouth. Feeling safe, Ivy reached up to touch his face. The boy flinched at first, but did not sense any danger. As she cupped his cheek in her hand, he moved his head against it, enjoying the contact and the sensation of warm, soft skin.

"Hello," she whispered, and with a sudden movement away from her hand, they were face to face, noses almost touching. Ivy felt nervous, a knot in her stomach – not out of fear or danger, but another reason she could not understand. He had not spoken to her, and she wondered whether he could, but she was sure there was a mutual communication. He was, after all, human, and she again broke their eye contact to look at the muscular strength of his torso and the power in his thighs. His hand closed around her forearm, gently, but with control. Ivy watched as he brought his other hand, greenish against the clear sky, to her cheek, then her chin, the nape of her neck, until the knot in her stomach tightened and she blurted out, "Who are you?"

At this, the boy dropped his hands and shuffled backwards. Ivy instinctively held out her hands, palms flat, as a sign of safety.

"I'm sorry," she said softly. "I'm sorry." She pondered what to say next. "My name is Ivy." He blinked. She pointed at herself. "Ivy". Did he nod? "I live in Fenwood." She pointed behind her. The boy rose up on his haunches and peered over her in the direction her hand motioned. Ivy brushed her falling brown hair away from her face, enthused by the degree of understanding. In an instant his head jerked to the right. His body tensed. "What is it?" she asked, forgetting that there would be no response. He was motionless. Ivy craned her head to look in the same direction but could see nothing, just a screen of patchy grass, wild shrubbery and low-hanging boughs. "Wha—" but she was cut short as the boy turned his gaze back to her, studied her for a moment as if contemplating, and in a single motion, turned and bolted along the path and into the undergrowth, away from unseen danger. Ivy was dumbstruck; the speed at which he had departed and the way in which he had seemed to unsettle not even a leaf, as if the natural foliage had parted for him. Who was he? What was he doing here? Where was he going? She was aware that her heart was beating rapidly. The boy-beast had aroused in her more raw emotion and life than anything she could remember. Brushing down her cotton dress, the princess once again looked out across the pool. A fire lit in her soul.

*   *   *

The Queen turned her back on the courtyard, its familiar noises and smells, and headed back into the stone-walled corridors. Where was that girl? Ivy had an uncommonly good knack of not being found. Increasingly so, of late.

She shook her head and regretted the declining relationship between them. It had been the same between her and her mother. Yet she had grown to enjoy the ceremony and sense of tradition. Ivy hadn't and probably never would. Her will…

Deep in thought, the Queen collided with a young serving boy who hurried toward the courtyard with a cloth over his arm. Startled in the realisation of who he had run into, he fell almost to his knees, bowing and mumbling apologies, distraught at his accidental mishap. The lady had not fallen but doubled over at the waist, coughing wildly. It was some moments before she regained her composure and her breathing.

"It's ok, no harm done," the Queen reassured him, placing her hand on his arm to straighten him up. He gasped at her touch and she in turn laughed at his adulation. "Now, by way of an apology, you can help me." He nodded, still stunned. "I need you to find my daughter and tell her to meet me in the Hall of Ceremonies. Can you do that?" He nodded again. Stroking his cheek, the Queen thanked him and moved on down the corridor.

The poor boy stood still, struck with the awful choice of lying to the Queen or betraying Ivy, who he had seen heading toward the secret door in the West flank of the oaks.

*   *   *

The chance encounter with the boy brought Ivy to the forest with greater regularity. She wanted to see him again, yes, but there was also a sense of peace and beauty and understanding there beneath the wooded canopy that she did not feel anywhere else. Not only did she enjoy the breezed whispers of the trees and the luscious, enlivened colours of the forest, the pool itself was unlike any place she had ever experienced. It was as if she could feel the water, the stones, the trees all singing, all in harmony, and she was such an insignificant yet somehow necessary part of that song.

The wild boy was nowhere to be seen, although she was starkly aware that she had only wandered a little way into the grand expanse of the forest. He must live somewhere, but she knew not where. Her mind had floated away from the morning table, her physik lessons and dress rehearsals for some pointless ceremony, to the forest and to him. There was so much that she wished to find out about him, and from him: about the forest, the lands beyond, how all these living things were interconnected. Yet, as she stood with her back to the opening of the green-boughed cavernous entrance, Ivy knew that there was a strong chance she would never see him again.

"You know your mother would be so disappointed to know that you are abandoning your duties to play explorers in the forest," came a voice, oozing around the undergrowth. She half expected to see Laurent, but the sound was far more sickly-sweet than his callous tones. Shaken from her thoughts, she stepped carefully forward. Rukmahl leaned against a sturdy trunk, biting ferociously into an apple that crunched in defeat.

"Mr Rukmahl. What brings you out from your lair? Bored of your luxuries?"

He smiled at the retort. Clearly the girl had wit.

"Me? Oh, I am merely concerned with your welfare, and therefore the welfare of this fair city." Crunch. "I would hate for something to…" Crunch "…happen to you."

"Your concern is noted," Ivy replied with forced formality, and she moved to go around him. Rukmahl pushed himself away from the tree, shifting his weight to his feet.

"The forest is full of dangers, little girl." He leaned down towards her, suddenly imposing himself. "Your mother ails. Can your slight shoulders carry the burden of a whole city?" He smirked at her obvious discomfort. "I can help y—" He broke off with a cry of pain, clutching the fleshy folds of his cheek. A second compacted mud-rock flew from the undergrowth and exploded against the opposite side of his temple. He screamed in rage. No discernible words were formed, just a growl, and he blundered forward to the spot where the missiles had been fired. He tore at the leaves and scrubs. There was nothing there.

"DO YOU KNOW WHO I AM?!" he raged. "I'LL KILL YOU, YOU MISERABLE BEAST! I'LL TEAR YOUR HIDE FROM YOUR BONES!" Turning back to Ivy, wary of a setup, he barked, "Did you know ab…" But she had gone, fleeing from his beastly company.

(iv)

The pool had watched the tentative meeting and nervous fumblings of the children, rejoicing in a union it had long known was right.

It would protect them when they needed it.

But they must overcome. Together.

The wind swept through the trees and water with a collective sigh. Were the children strong enough?

CHAPTER 9

A CRY FOR HELP

For the third time in four new suns, the Queen coughed herself awake from a fitful slumber; violent coughs that sent her throat into spasm. One hand shot to hold her neck in the vain hope that it would help, whilst the other bony hand flailed for the floral embroidered cotton handkerchief by her bedside. She rolled onto her side and vomited phlegm into the handkerchief. As her breath returned, she opened the delicate square in her hand. Blood. Blood on the flowers and reeds. A sign of things to come. Her body was shaking, her pillow drenched in sweat, and now this. Still trying to control her breathing, she reached a trembling hand out and grabbed the sticky bottle that sat in a small puddle on the wooden stand.

Putting it to her lips, she squeezed her eyes together at the now familiar burning sensation in her throat as she swallowed it. He had assured her it was natural due to the presence of mustard seed in the tonic. Despite all of Rukmahl's remedies and kind advice, she could only see herself getting worse. How long did she have left? Not long enough. Ivy. She wasn't ready yet.

Clutching a woven tapestry in her trembling hand, she drew it back to let the early light flood into the room; once it had given her vigour for the day ahead, but now she shielded her eyes. Turning away from the light, she rang the rope bell that hung by her bedside. Within seconds a calm knocking rattled on the chamber door, followed by a gruff, friendly, "Morning, ma'am." The frail lady shuffled across the room, and opened the creaking door to reveal the aged, sunken eyes of Ernest's weatherworn face. As he smiled, his eyes all but disappeared beneath the wrinkles.

"Ernest. Please... Please don't tell me you've been out here all night?" the Queen asked with loving reproach. Ernest's eyes dropped to the floor.

"Umm... No, m'lady, I... erm... I was, by chance, just passing..." Even though he looked up again, he could not hold her gaze. For a moment the Queen wondered what it would be like to spend her life with a man like Ernest, and the thought was surprisingly warming to her heart. She smiled again.

"Your wife was a very lucky lady, Ernest."

The old man's eyes dropped again, but this time to hide his emotion rather than his lies. She took his hand in hers and squeezed gently. "Bring Mr Rukmahl to me please, Ernest."

His movement was sudden and instinctive.

"But ma'am, this early?" His eyes this time were lost in a furrowed brow. The Queen tried to soften him again with a smile.

"Please, Ernest." She pulled her hand away, but his bony fingers held onto hers.

"Ma'am, you shouldn't…"

"Ernest, please."

But he was determined.

"Ma'am, can I speak freely?"

"Ernest, can you—"

"I know you think he's helping you, but he isn't." And suddenly Ernest's eyes were on her with real concern – no, panic, written into the worldly creases of his face. "Please," he continued. "Please listen to me – many years I have cared for you, m'lady, and now I see you making, excuse me… such terrible decisions—"

"Ernest, stop—"

"—and relying on this man who just seeks to use

you—"

"Stop, Ernest."

"—and then cast you aside, without a care for your health at all—"

"Ernest…"

"—or for whether you live or die—"

"STOP!" And the coughing returned. Bent double, clutching her stomach, the coughs ripped through her chest and throat, depriving her of breath. Tears tumbled down her face, and phlegm and vomit fell from her mouth to the floor.

Ernest was dumbstruck. All his years and experience of servitude rendered helpless by fear, horror and guilt. He became aware that other people had arrived, bodies around him supporting the weak lady in front of him and even talking at him, but he could not hear. A hand grabbed him around the upper arm, and he looked into the world-weary eyes of Chief Tindal. The man's voice was a formless echo, a vibration with no discernible words. Ernest nodded instinctively, unaware of the instruction or question that had come his way, and the guard turned his attention to the Queen, leaving the servant to attempt to recover his sense of self. Ernest turned and with back stooped, legs trembling, balance unsteady, trundled into the imposing shadows of the castle corridors.

*   *   *

"But, needless to say, the cherumin berries that I practically risked my life to pick were what actually saved his life, and even though he offered me the woodland as a reward, I declined as salvaging his life was reward enough for me." The story was completed with a simple and modest smile, and met with complete adoration, infatuation and desire from its wide-eyed, transfixed audience. For them it was like drinking in the sweetest and smoothest honey mead just to hear his advice, his stories, and to be merely in his company.

Rukmahl's morning 'group therapy session' had begun as an opportunity, once every seven suns, for people of the castle and of noble repute to have their issues and ailments discussed by the gilded tongue of the wise man (although to begin with, people had come more from intrigue than need). However, they became so popular and abundantly attended that they became more frequent – Rukmahl himself did not seem to mind as, for him, it meant greater access to the castle, the Queen, and to adoring 'patients'. The attendants had quickly evolved into entirely female groups. Women would spend many an hour preparing themselves for their morning with the large grotesquely garbed man; whether married or single, they competed for his words, the cupping of his hand when he gave advice, or the brush of his beard against their face when he consoled. It was also known that, for those in dire need, Rukmahl would offer private visitations in the rooms he had been granted in the castle; these could be quick visits or run for many hours into the night (depending on the money that could be exchanged, or the sheer need of the patient).

Despite his pompousness, his arrogance and the sense of vulnerability he provoked in people, he was completely trusted by nearly all the city. He spoke with such authority, he commanded such attention, and his growing importance in the castle meant that his influence grew across Fenwood. It had begun with pharmacy and medicine, but now worthy citizens sought his opinions on finance, relationships and fashion. The air of mystery he maintained surrounding his personal life only enhanced his reputation for wisdom, this velvet-tongued stranger who had experience of all from lands afar. And as the Queen became increasingly withdrawn from the daily life of her beloved people, with questions and rumours spreading as to her health or commitment, Rukmahl's star shone ever brighter.

It was this very notion he sat reflecting upon in the

comfort of his private consultation room, cigar rolling between his rounded fingers, gazing out at the wisteria, a vibrant pink against the blue sky. A self-satisfied smile wrung his lips.

"Mr Rukmahl?" came a tense voice from the opposite sofa. He had forgotten his clients: a couple experiencing marital problems. He turned his bulky back to them.

"I am smiling, Mr and Mrs Crumpton, because there is obviously a deep love that still burns between you both" – blank, grey faces gazed back – "and it is important that you make time for each other, away from the baking oven—"

"I'm a ceramics maker," interjected the uncomfortable man opposite; a flash of irritation crossed Rukmahl's face, which quickly fell to a slobbering smile.

"Well, of course, pottery baking oven, I meant," he forced through his curved mouth, before continuing. "Mr Crumpton, I want you to head to my dispensary and ask for a bottle of Vedandum, which I have brewed especially for you, sir. It will cost you, no doubt, but it will create a greater sense of confidence in yourself and your ability to keep your wife content in the home. Mrs Crumpton, if you would but wait here for a small time, I will impart to you some techniques that the folk of the Western Isles use for maintaining a happy, loving relationship." He was aware that the look that had materialised on his face might be giving away his inner pleasure, so adjusting the corners of his smile, he projected the intended innocence for the gullible pair.

*   *   *

For some days now Ernest had felt like the only person really caring for Mother, and the only person who saw the blasted apothecary for the master manipulator he truly was. Yet as he looked down at the frail, once regal lady who convulsed and grimaced with pain, he could feel no choice but to comply with her wishes. Yes, she pleaded with her words, but it was the panic and fear in her eyes that rendered him defenceless. His irregular footsteps echoed against the cold, stone walls and suddenly it hit him that he was very much alone in his thoughts, support and position. Ernest slowed and steadied himself with one hand on the brick, catching his breath, both from age and realisation.

"Ivy," he muttered to the shadows. Where was the child? Who was caring for her? Who was preparing her for her responsibilities when… when… He coughed the thoughts from his head and once more took up his enforced task.

*   *   *

"Now, Mrs Appleby, if you keep your eyes closed and breathe in deeply…" oozed Rukmahl, bending over the defenceless lady with a smoking vial under her nose. With her eyes closed she could not see the engorged face scanning down her body. The weak knock on the door broke his concentration.

"I'm in a consultation!" he snapped through gritted teeth, and then swung his head up slowly, like a disturbed predator, as the door opened anyway. The Queen's servant stood there, stooped with fatigue, but with a look of indignation on his wrinkled face. Rukmahl suppressed the eagerness that flared inside.

"Oh, I am so sorry, Mrs Appleby," crooned the alchemist, with a sickly look of a wounded puppy on his face, "but I believe I have a royal calling." He quickly bundled the buxom woman out of the room with many unfelt apologies and a promise of further consultation soon. Ernest stopped the door from closing.

"Our Mother has requested you," he said, trying to sound authoritative. "I can only hope that your concern is for her health and not the furthering of your career."

Rukmahl smiled. He walked over to his desk, gown billowing behind him, where several bottles stood, and he carefully fingered each.

"It is not me you hate, old man, it is the fact that she needs me, not you," he said menacingly without even looking up. "And besides, it is not hatred. It is jealousy." With the final barbed statement, he turned swiftly so that his large stomach rippled beneath the many fabrics of his garments, just to catch a glimpse of the wrath folding into the elderly servant's face. The large, grotesque figure walked towards the elder man slowly, ominously. Holding up a vial between thumb and forefinger, he goaded Ernest.

"Do you know what this is, old man?"

The servant shook his head but could not put sound to the word 'no' on his lips. Rukmahl merely laughed. "Exactly." Their shoulders clashed as the alchemist charged from the room, barely feeling the contact whilst the servant fell into the door frame, whimpering as he stopped himself from hitting the floor.

*   *   *

She had just caught her breath when the next one came. This time it began as a stabbing sensation in her chest and lungs before the inevitable fire burning up her throat and the violent, hacking bark that erupted from her mouth, forcing her whole body forward. Her hands clutched the edge of the heavy, oaken dressing table, turning her knuckles white. Wave after wave of lurching coughs followed and with every one the Queen wondered if this would be her last expulsion of breath. But they did subside. Looking up, the ageing lady's wrinkled and haggard face gazed back from the mirror between the splatters of blood-flecked phlegm. The eyes that once danced sat sunken in hollow caves, dead, with the wracked body ready to follow.

All the while, Rukmahl had waited outside the door, patiently, for the coughing to pass; he had carefully cleaned the green residue from beneath his fingernails and admired the skill with which the young man with the beautiful skin had applied the lacquer… What had been his name, now? As he pondered, he gave the polished door knob a twist and opened the door. The Queen's back was to him as she supported herself on the dressing table. He could see the rise and fall of her frail shoulders as she struggled to regain her breathing. Those luxuriant, regal gowns now hung from her body like expensive peasant's sacks – he smiled to himself at the irony of this, as his own garments grew ever tighter on his indulged, bulking frame. She was, however, still alive, and that in itself showed considerable fight in the old girl.

"Ma'am," he offered in his sickliest voice. She began to

turn, but her legs were not ready to support her weight yet and she crumbled from the thighs down; knees buckling inwards, feet sliding on the flagstones, left arm sweeping along the thick oak and sending vials, phials and bottles crashing to the floor along with the Queen's ragged body in a cacophony of noise. Rukmahl's hand shot to his mouth, a gesture of shock that hid the riotous grin that threatened to spread across his face. He bumbled across the room to her and knelt at her side. She was weeping. He took her fragile fingers in his enormous hand, engulfing her. Without looking up, she whispered through her tears, "My dear friend… How did it come to this?" She was shaking. He placed his hand on her chest, a gesture that should have shown tenderness but seemed oppressive. Rukmahl looked at her and narrowed his eyes; she was searching for words to say, and he sensed they were the words he had waited so long, and worked so hard, to hear.

"Shh, Mother, don't speak," he said mockingly.

Her skeletal hand clutched his immense arm.

"Please," she stuttered through cries. "Please." She paused. "Help me." She gave a choke. "Help my people."

*   *   *

Ivy sat on the petrified tree stump. Her outstretched hand

held scraps of meat from last night's hog roast, carried from the celebratory dinner under a cloth. She barely moved; the rise and fall of her chest, breathing deeply but silently, the only sign of life. Opposite, sniffing the air, the boy looked quizzically at the morsels in her hand. Forward he crawled, secure in his instinct of safety. His glaze flickered to her eyes and back to the items in her hand. Sniffing again. Food. Then an unfurled grasp, drawing a sliver of meat to his lips. Sniff. Placed to his lips. Good. Chewing. A smile of enjoyment spread across his entire face. Ivy could not help but smile too, a warm sensation rising from her stomach to her face.

"More?" she offered. "Have the rest. Yummy."

The boy seemed to understand and took the remainder, staying near her. Again, she felt the desire to touch him and put her hand to his cheek. This time he did not flinch.

"How did you get here?" she wondered aloud. He laid his head to one side, studying her, the look on his face suggesting he was considering who she was too. And suddenly he took her hand. She gasped momentarily before being led through the light brush, carefully, protectively. She followed without question, relishing the interaction. They had not gone far when the boy came to a stop, not in a clearing but where the canopy of trees opened to the cloudy sky and, in the distance, the castle tower. Making sure she was looking at him, the boy extended his smudged arm and pointed at the tower.

"Yes, castle," Ivy tried, wanting to help the communication. "Tower?"

His face showed signs of frustration and a low, gruff growl sounded in his throat as he dropped his head. Looking up again he pointed at Ivy and then at the castle.

"Oh, yes! That is where I'm from!" she erupted in delight. "You remembered," she said, more softly, almost to herself. He grinned, half at his own success and half at having pleased her. "And you?" she followed up, pointing at him. "Where?" and she raised her hands up in question. His head moved to the side, thinking. Ivy expected him to point or to take her somewhere, but instead he reached down and grabbed a handful of earth, grass and leaves. Holding out his hands he gesticulated she do the same and preceded to pour the contents into hers. She considered the natural debris, and understood.

The pool sensed them first, before the trees uttered their names. Footsteps thudding along the hallowed roads. A detestable rhythm.

> *Thud. Thud. Thud.*
> *Gold. Gold. Gold.*
> *Doom. Doom. Doom.*

But the pool kept faith with the children, as the boughs of trees closed protectively closer around its still waters.

CHAPTER 10

THE COMING OF THE WISE

The large, bejewelled alchemist had told the people they would come in ten days. They were three days late.

"I have called in favours of great men from distant lands, men who have experience of governing great cities," Rukmahl had told them. He had called an assembly, not at the market place but at the gates of the castle. He had kept them waiting, crowding around the ornate stonework pillars, and peering through gaps between heads. When finally, the heavy wooden doors had groaned open, he looked almost ridiculous in purple velvet and animal pelt. He had addressed them with arms outstretched, voice flowing through the people like a river of wine through rocks of ice. And they had listened, drinking it in.

"They will come in ten days, Gods willing. Your Mother ails…" At this there was an audible disturbance and muttering. "I have tended to her day by day, but alas the sickness that has taken hold of her is sweeping her up in its cold embrace and not relinquishing its grasp." He bowed his head and when he looked up, the people could see tears in his eyes. "She is… beyond my skill to heal." 'How could that be?', they thought. "I can fight illness… but I cannot defeat death." Gasps. He paused. Even he was impressed by his own performance. "At such times it is necessary to pass on the reign to the next of kin, but Ivy is too young, too naïve, and…" He swept his arm around. "Too absent." The people nodded – the girl was seldom seen these days. He continued, "I have advised a good many of you in recent times, and now I beg that you listen to my advice once more. I have asked for good, honest men to help us in our hour of need." Here he took a step forward and made eye contact with individuals, drawing them in. "Our work rotas need drawing up, the crops need reaping, the waters need blessing. Traditions MUST be upheld!" he roared with orchestrated passion. And applause rang around him.

Long after his crescendo, Rukmahl's sweetened words drifted around the corners of the city. Helpless individuals could be seen hovering, loitering, grovelling by the gates in the Oaken Ring. The castle walls were not crumbling, the crops were not failing, but the good people felt leaderless, a ship adrift in the night, lacking a focal figure. On the occasions that Rukmahl hauled himself to the gate, they would fawn at his robe tails, begging him to stand forth and lead. They mistook his greedy smiles for pity and did not see the mocking as he peered through the door's viewing window.

"Alas, I am not fit for rule," he would say, absorbing the compliments that were thrown his way.

"My dear, I am not of this city," he would parrot, never revealing where his roots lay.

"You are so kind, sweet one," he would pour with a lascivious eye, "but come to my chambers in an hour to make your plea."

Days passed.

Weeks.

Patch, the weaver's serving boy (who coincidentally bore a birthmark over his left eye), clambered up the moss-strewn steps that ran to the viewing platform over the trunk layer of the oaken pillars either side of the door. Reaching the top, he let out a steadying breath and brushed the stone dust from his tatty knees. Looking up he noticed a forlorn lady waiting patiently at the top of the steps. She let out a sigh.

"No good, little one. Don't waste your playtime."

Patch gave an embarrassed look, frowned at the unspecific animal design on her smock and brushed past the lady, who descended slowly down the steps. Perching on tiptoes and squinting comically, the boy could see into the distance through a gap in the leaves. Nothing. Emptiness. Countless trees. A horse. Two horses. Three. With riders. More. He looked away and blinked. When he looked back, he could clearly see an entourage, of how many he could not tell, moving towards Fenwood. Men on horseback. Wagons. Servants. It was them.

They were coming. Fenwood was saved.

*   *   *

The boy's large brown eyes broke from his gaze upon Ivy's lips as she talked, sniffing the air in an agitated manner.

"What is it?" Ivy asked, urgency in her voice at his change of mood. He sniffed again, furtively. He grabbed her arm as if it were an emergency, pulling her after him as he half bounded, half ran towards a point that only he seemed to know. Ivy stumbled after him, tripping in his wake.

As they reached the forest edge, slowing his pace, the boy gesticulated to Ivy that she should quieten; only then did she realise that she was inhaling and exhaling loudly, out of breath. Pulling her in close, his rough hands caressed the curtain of branches aside. Not far in front of them they observed the passing of the train: figures robed in simple yet expensive fabrics, shades of wise white and grey hair, walked or rode on wooden carts laden with chests and casques containing who knew what. Wary brown eyes turned back to her. She sensed that these men and their cavalcade thought their arrival a cause for great celebration in the city; to the reluctant princess it seemed more like an ominous funeral march.

*   *   *

The cumbersome oaken doors had been opened well before the entourage had arrived. A crowd had assembled and more were coming, with many people holding offerings of food, crafts and, in some cases, jewels. But none were taken, for these were the Wise. Their arrival was not in a cloak of secrecy and stealth in the night, but heralded by fanfares, flanked by the folk of Fenwood thanking them and appealing for the assistance that had not come from their absent Mother in many months.

Twelve men entered the city, hailed as saviours and redeemers, mysterious and exalted. Many of the simple folk noticed how unadorned and rough their clothing was, a stark contrast to the man who had summoned them. The Wise did not look down to make eye contact, but nodded and waved with crooked fingers as they passed silently by. As the procession continued, carts began wheeling, creaking through the gates; those lining the streets dared to wonder what riches and marvels were stowed inside. Carts were closely followed by servants who held their heads high in dignity and arrogance. But Fenwood did not notice or care about the upturn of noses. They saw only the simple upturn of fortune. The gathering crowd now formed a melee that threatened to spill over with excitement and relief into the road. Somewhere, crude music stuttered into life, and the grotesque carnival was complete.

From his panoramic castle window. Rukmahl watched all with devilish glee. The constructed joy. The undetected plan. Pawns in his game of chess. He wiped the beef dripping from his mouth with his cravat. He should probably go and say something profound, he mused.

Ensconced in the archway of Guards' Gate, Chief Tindal leant on the old stone, running his hand unconsciously over the royal crest emblazoned on his armour. He knew, with each cart that passed him, these men were not here to save Fenwood. They were not the solution. Merely adding to the problem. These men with their knotted hands and selfish minds would ransack Fenwood of its traditions and resources. And what could he, Tindal, do? Follow orders, as he had done his whole life. As the final cart rumbled past on the dirt track, he rubbed his stubbled face with his rough hand. He was tired. The feeling that lingered at the tail end of the procession was not anger or vengeance, but sadness. Deep sadness for the Queen and Ivy, for the honest and vulnerable people and children who had been mis-sold hope. Sadness for the city he loved. His hand came to rest, as it often did, on the hilt of his sword. The blade of protection and justice. In his heart he knew it would still be needed, one way or another.

On the other side of the great white stone building, from her floor-level basement window, Mrs Maltcross looked up and frowned.

"Gods have mercy," she muttered. Nobody had told her there would be twelve plus servants. She slung a towel over her shoulder and headed into the belly of the building.

Ivy knew she should return to the castle. Not to welcome the council or celebrate the apparent 'saving' of Fenwood, but to be amongst the people and support her mother. As the wooden doors clanged shut behind the final load-bearing cart Ivy exhaled deeply. A clear sense of where she was flooded over her and she felt the rough, warm hand of the boy in hers. In that moment, so fleeting and effortless, a choice was unthinkingly made.

"Come," Ivy whispered, crouching to his squatted level, "show me your home."

CHAPTER 11

THE COUNCIL

In truth, the arrival of the council was met with a vast range of opinion and feeling. Yes, there was joy and thanksgiving that such notable and noble sirs would travel such a way to offer their wisdom and guidance. Some, however, questioned who these men were, why they would offer their help, and what they would want in return. Nevertheless, a largely jubilant and curious crowd gathered and ushered the aged men into the white stone castle. The men waved and nodded to the crowds, but offered no words of welcome or thanks. The mass of onlookers waited for some time, craning their necks for glances at windows and narrowing their eyes for an appearance at a rampart. There was no sign. Disappointed, the people slowly drifted away back to the normality of simple life. Many glanced up at the clouds that gathered above their heads. Rain was on its way.

*   *   *

As the castle gates had closed behind the caravan of guests, carts and luggage, it was Rukmahl who had greeted them in the courtyard. He had waited with eyes full of wonder and opportunity until they had all come to a standstill. Then nodded.

"Thank you, gentlemen, for coming." Silence, drinking it all in. "Your journey here will be well rewarded." An ageing man with a carved walking stick shuffled forwards.

"I am Master Blastington. Thank you for summoning us. There is much we can do here." Rukmahl studied him for a few seconds, hurt by the interruption, but did not reply. Beckoning to the shadows, several castle servants appeared and began busying themselves with the carrying of bags and boxes, the housing of horses, the stowing of carriages. Only Ernest remained hidden behind a stone pillar. Rukmahl spoke again, more formally this time.

"If you will follow me, please, my good sirs. We have much business to attend to. The Great Hall has been prepared for us."

There was very little talk as the men filed into the grand mahogany-panelled hall, decked on all sides with paintings, trinket-covered sideboards and long-forgotten coats of arms. Carved, cushioned chairs were scraped on the flagstones as the councilmen tucked themselves under the imposing round oaken table in the centre of the room. Bearded mouths turned and muttered to one another, a mumbled hubbub in an otherwise stifling quiet.

"Gentlemen."

Suddenly, there was silence.

The eyes of the solemn men turned to the head of the table where the commanding figure of Rukmahl had placed himself. His excessive lifestyle now displayed its signs on the exuberant man's body, and he shifted his additional weight in the sunken cushion of the chair. Once adjusted, he exhaled purposefully; each shallow eye remained fixed upon him and now he returned each look, meeting each man's gaze. Finally, once every man had been drawn in, he dropped his searching eyes to the table and simply, softly, nodded.

For the next few months, Rukmahl and the men of the council orchestrated and ordered Fenwood from the stable luxury of the castle. Occasionally the large, gaudy extrovert would be seen in the streets, or wandering the market place, or socialising at the inn. The figure-head. The mouth-piece. The charm offensive. Behind the scenes the bearded old men did what they knew best: drew up charters, logged percentages, allocated targets. The liberal collective of Fenwood became a machine. Rukmahl continued to stoke the embers of invasion with vague threats and allusions of collapse; fear-mongering and preying on the vulnerabilities of a people who hung on his every word. His plan was being borne out with such ease, such wanton perfection. It would only be a matter of time before they would turn on themselves and he could lead this so-called *city* to… progress. There was but one thorn in his intent.

And so it was that, months later, Rukmahl found himself once again hauling his bulk from the flattened cushions of the ornate, Great Hall chair, to stand ahead the table, addressing the beady and clouded eyes of the council.

"Gentlemen." The murmurs died. "I want to congratulate, and thank, you all. What we have achieved here is the beginning of something wonderful… no, strike that…" He paused, shutting his eyes to grasp the word in the darkness. "Something majestic."

The wrinkled, cracked faces formed into smiles, straining muscles that had long since been forgotten.

"This town, well, *village*" – the tone brought muffled snorts of laughter – "was rotting, like the wooden beams that held it together. It was wasting away, flooded with ineptitude and sluggishness, drowning in a sea of liberal-minded, false idol worship." Nods of approval, hands slapping on veneered mahogany and a lonesome, "Hear, hear!"

"We have stopped that rot. We have stemmed the tide of patheticism. We have introduced a new life and vigour. This *village* is now a town, and, with your help, will be a city; a jewel in this crowned land. Productivity will be far beyond what we could have hoped or dreamt of—"

"It is already up one hundred and twelve per cent," came a voice from the far end of the table. A silence followed. Rukmahl glared at the balding man, his stride broken. Something of a mumbled apology escaped the man's lips and he recoiled into his chair. Rukmahl continued.

"Productivity has risen dramatically, tumbledown community buildings have been reinforced and general order has been restored at a time when the sovereignty has disintegrated through illness." On the word 'illness', Rukmahl's eyes glinted with well-hidden meaning. The aged faces around the carved table reflected the self-satisfaction that emanated from the table head. But now the leathered brow crumpled and a storm floated in.

"However, gentlemen, a loose end remains; a weakness, an innocent and uncontemplated core." The men's eyes nervously flicked back and forth, searching for the elusive component. Blastington craned his neck and shoulders forward and croaked.

"The girl?" All eyes turned looked at him and then back to the engorged focal figure.

"The girl." Rukmahl let out another, more troubled breath. "The girl is a reminder to the gormless people of this ignorant town of a time that was, not what is and what will be. She cannot be allowed to reignite the flames in those pure hearts. She must be... dealt with."

"If I may speak?" interjected a voice belonging to grey eyes that pierced from under heavy black eyebrows. "It has been reported to us that the girl spends ever longer away from the town and its people, in the company of a boy. My questioning is double-edged: is she, surely, no longer a threat, having been significantly isolated? And if not, what danger is the boy she draws solace from?"

Rukmahl nodded with self-assured forethought.

"You are correct, my friend, to raise such issues, and I thank you for your *wise* contribution" – at this he glanced at the younger, bald man who still reeled back in his chair – "I have tracked the boy and learnt as much of him as can be told. He is nothing but a child of the forest and merely a matter of curiosity to the people, but of little significance. Whilst the princess has indeed appeared to turn her back on her people and those who love her, she is nevertheless a focal point, a touchstone, around which Fenwood can gather. I will not risk all that has been, and will be, achieved here on a whimsical notion that she is so enamoured with this… this boy, that she will not return. Ladies' minds are fickle traps, gentlemen. I want to be sure. I want this dealt with."

There was a hush. Outside, the sounds of men calling to each other in the fields could be faintly heard, and slowly raindrops began pattering on the window as storm clouds drifted in once again. Rukmahl's words were the narration of his inner thoughts, but rung like orders inside the heads of the council members. The silence in the room became thick and uncomfortable.

"What, then, is to be done?" uttered the heavy-browed man. A smile flashed across Rukmahl's eyes.

"We must be kept distant from any *eventualities*; we cannot be implicated in whatever happens to the girl. An accident perhaps?"

"A hired hand?" came a ragged voice.

"Cannot be trusted not to rat us out, even if paid well enough." Thought showed in Rukmahl's crystal blue eyes.

"No, we need someone we can manipulate; a weak fool with a weaker mind who will carry out any plans such as we can manoeuvre into the thoughts of our disastrous puppet."

Again, the crimson smile tainting the two pools peered at the faces around the table. They waited for his next word in hushed silence. Distant cries could be heard. Rain began to hammer on the rattling pane. Then the sound of a door handle turning, thickset oak hitting wooden bookshelves as the door was flung open, and crackled gasps from withering throats.

And he entered. Whether by fate or coincidence, Laurent stood in the doorway to the room, holding a tray of precariously balanced glasses of barley water, hand still outstretched having lost control of the opening door. Frozen in startled terror, he looked around at the gaunt faces that gazed at his innocently contorted face. He stammered before mumbling nervously, "Your drinks, gentlemen."

Rukmahl rose to welcome the servant.

*   *   *

The glasses sat empty on the table in front of the satisfied councillors. The door swung shut behind the loping gait of the trusting serving boy. The men waited until the door clicked in the catch of the door frame, and even though they did not speak, the tension eased. Almost as one, they rose from the table, as did the overbearing figure at its head. He spoke softly now, pacing slowly around the table and shaking each man's hand.

"Thank you, gentlemen. Ever is your wisdom a comfort and a need in these testing times. We must all still be vigilant." He reached the man with the deep-set eyes, placing his other hand onto the handshake to show his appreciation, accompanied with a nod. He moved on.

"But for now, the wheels are set in motion, and we must remain patient." He stopped. "We must succeed."

The men gave nods of approval and shuffled towards the door.

"Oh, and Grieves…" All the councillors hesitated, but the balding man took a step in Rukmahl's direction.

"Sir?"

The sound of Rukmahl's hand across Grieves' face resounded off the archaic cabinets and dusty panelled walls. Blazing red finger marks appeared almost instantaneously on his cheek. The balding man stumbled and fell to the ground; Rukmahl glowered over him.

"Don't ever interrupt me again."

The immense figure turned back to face the window

and was quickly left alone.

CHAPTER 12

EGAN

Ivy slunk into the shadow beside the door frame. The cold stone wall on her back made her gasp, stifled by a quick hand to cover her mouth. Inside the room she could hear Mr Kitterton's crisp voice bemoaning the princess' lack of attendance at the rehearsal for... for what, Ivy could not remember. She waited until the Master's voice drifted to one side and she took the chance to creep past the doorway, tiptoeing almost silently down the hallway. The far door opened noiselessly, and she sighed with relief in the corridor beyond.

"Going out?" croaked a barbed voice from the gloom of the corner. Ivy squinted her eyes. She could make out the outline of an irregular human form. As it materialised from the darkness the form became Laurent. Ivy stared at him, annoyed, disturbed by his presence.

"Are you going to see *him*?" There was a real bitterness in the final word, spat through gritted teeth.

"That's none of your business," Ivy coldly fired back, rearing her body back in defiance.

"It's my job to look out f…" Laurent began.

"Your job? I'm a job?" Ivy goaded.

"No, that's not what I meant. I…"

"I've always endured your company on our walks. Your company meant nothing to me." She knew it would sting, and she wanted it to. "I'll say it again, my life is none of your business. I don't want you near me again."

"Ivy, I'm sorry, I just don't want you to get hurt. You have your duties to look to and…"

"NONE OF YOUR BUSINESS," she yelled. The moment lingered. "Now get out of my way." Reluctantly he shuffled ashamedly to one side. Ivy pushed passed him, pausing only momentarily to turn and sneer, "And it is 'm'lady' to you". The door slammed on Laurent as he cowered.

*   *   *

Ivy watched the boy. Transfixed. A half smile, partly

novelty, partly sheer joy, etched into her face. The way that he sniffed and licked things. The movements of his head and hands. The crude but natural interactions with the world around him. The natural world. His world. And he was beginning to allow Ivy in.

At first, he had cowered and darted suspiciously at each of her movements, continually eyeing her with caution. Yet he had not run away or given primitive suggestion that he wished her gone. Caution then gave way to intrigue. For a time they walked together in the dense forest, beyond boundaries – Ivy's pace slow and careful beside her companion's animalistic reliance on four limbs. At a certain tree, thick with an emerald green moss, the forest-child had stopped and indicated she do the same with a punctuated exhalation. He curled the moss between his fingers and, yanking, tore a clump from its grip on the bark. Offering it to her, Ivy accepted the gift warmly. Only when he gesticulated his undergrowth-smudged hand to his mouth did she balk, before regaining her composure and remembering her etiquette training. Managing to hide the uncertainty and disgust, she raised the tangled moss to her mouth. It tasted exactly how she expected moss to taste: unpleasant to a palette raised on refined food. But she saw in his eyes a warmth that came from acceptance.

His communication began as grunts and growls,

accompanied by facial expressions and gesticulations, but Ivy saw in his alteration of guttural noises a possibility.

"Leaf," she said, sounding the word clearly as he held up to her the smooth object plucked from a withered branch. As was customary now when taking on something new, he cocked his head to one side. "Leaf," she repeated, his mouth silently mirrored the shapes hers made.

"L…Liff…"

Ivy suppressed her excitement.

"Leaf," she said again. "L…eee…ff." He screwed his eyes in concentration.

"Leeeeeeff," he echoed. This time she could not hold back her smile.

"Good! Now… Leaf."

"L… Leaf."

She was amazed by how quickly the boy adapted to the sounds. It was almost as if it was not new at all, merely remembering something long buried. Undaunted and spurred on by the challenge, she picked up a stick.

As she left him soon after to return to the city, she looked back and observed his crouched form, half camouflaged in the wooden backdrop, watching her go.

Ivy found that, more and more frequently, her mind took her on paths outside the castle, indeed outside the city boundaries and deeper into the forest. The whispers of the leaves and branches, the babbling of the streams, the sighs and murmurs of the trees. It was a language that she did not understand, but she found it beautiful and compelling, surrounded by ages of mystery and lore. He spoke it… And suddenly he crawled into her thoughts again. The boy. She could picture each line of his face, so vivid that if he had a new debris smudge when she saw him, she noticed it instantly. The quirk of his sounds had grown to a yearning to understand how he spoke to the forest. She had begun to teach him her language so that he could tell her; just basic words, but he had picked them up so quickly as if they were distant recollections rather than a foreign tongue. The way he had smiled at the word 'tree', gently taking her hand…

"Ivy!" a stern voice snapped in her ear. "Where have you gone? You're not concentrating. Imagining one of your silly little walks?" The princess cast a sideways glance at the prickly, beetroot-coloured hag whose nose stuck out at an inappropriate proximity to her ear.

"Mrs Hawks… Pardon… Ma'am, there is nothing sil —"

THWACK. A light bamboo cane smarted into the small of her back.

"A lady does not answer back. And she keeps her back straight."

137

Some time later, Ivy gently rubbed her back, more at the memory of the sharp pain rather than any lasting hurt. Her eyes rose from the cacophony of jars and bottles and creams on her dressing table to the gilded mirror above. She looked absently at her natural curls falling across her forehead, brushing them aside with a sweep of her hand, but with no real attempt to present them in any way. Beyond the mirror her window looked out over the Oaken Ring and the lands stretching into the distance. Again, she found her mind wandering…

"I thought Mrs 'Hawkeye' had already reprimanded you for being absent-minded today, Princess?!" came a familiar voice behind her, but it occurred to her the tone resonated uncomfortably now.

"How… I've told you not to call me that, Laurent," she snapped back, deciding against engaging with him and how he had known about her etiquette lesson that morning. Laurent whimpered like a chastised puppy.

"I don't want to walk today," she said coldly, without turning to look at him. As it was, she missed the crestfallen look that crippled his face. Part hurt, part anger, part jealousy. The loyal creature opened and closed his mouth a number of times, attempting to form words that he could not give voice to.

"You can go now L—" But the sound of a door being

closed in an attempt to hide his bitterness clunked behind her.

*   *   *

Ivy's hand brushed tenderly over the leaves that seemed to reach welcomingly towards her. Looking back, she could still see the boughs of the great oak trees, but she was confident nobody had seen her slip away. She shifted the bag onto her other shoulder and let out a sigh, not of relief but of nervous excitement. A noise to her right startled her and quickly she looked for a bush or stump to hide behind, but the figure was not trying to surprise her, and the boy materialised from the colours of the forest. Ivy's smile was instant, and his eyes told the same story. No words passed. None were needed.

"I knew you'd be here." She blushed. He blinked then pointed at her.

"You…" He nodded. "For you." The gaze they held become too intense, though they knew not why.

"In," the boy croaked, finally turning his eyes towards the tree barricade. Ivy inhaled.

"Are you sure?" she whispered.

"No," he replied, but he smiled, aware that he was being humorous. Ivy smiled back and struggled to understand the emotion that suddenly flooded her stomach and heart.

"You will need these," she said and, swinging the bag from her shoulder, began drawing out clothing garments. The boy began to shuffle backwards. Ivy paused.

"If you want to see my world, you will need clothes." He looked into her eyes. "Please." Reaching out, she laid her hand on his grubbied palm. He did not move it, recognising the trust in her eyes. Cautiously, he nodded.

He traced his hands over the cold stone, feeling the damp that ran over the brickwork in the lower quarters. Curiously, he sniffed his fingers. Moss. He held them to his lips, and spat. Sneering, he turned back to Ivy.

"No... Not... Good," he uttered and pointed at his tongue. "Do not."

Ivy kept the look of amused bewilderment from her face. "Thank you. I hadn't planned on licking the walls." The boy could not understand her tone so moved on.

Ivy walked a few paces behind him, studying his movements, his furtive mannerisms, his oft-feral body language. When they had entered the long-forgotten door at the base of the scullery he had been his usual bowed self, using his hands and feet for propulsion and exploration. Yet now his back had straightened somewhat, and as she watched she noticed he occasionally rose to walking on two legs. She wondered silently as to the change in him. As they reached a crossing tunnel he dropped again to all fours, sniffing, flinching, looking this way and that. Ivy took a tentative step forward, ready to place a hand on his shoulder and suggest which corridor to take, when he made a sharp head movement to the left. He sniffed the air repeatedly, consciously, as if identifying something. Ivy found she was holding her breath. Slowly, he rose from his haunches, bent, but standing on two feet. Peering through the gloom of the darkened tunnel it seemed as if he was searching for something; something long forgotten or lost. Slowly his head turned back to Ivy, his eyes swimming with… she could not tell. Confusion? Fear? Revelation?

"What is it?" she whispered. There was no reply other than a jerking of his head back toward the passageway. "There's nothing down there," Ivy tried again. "Just some old storerooms." But he had clearly begun to take hesitant steps in the direction that drew him. She had not managed to convince him to wear shoes, and his bare feet now slapped hauntingly on the cold slabs of the floor.

Further along the passage he paused again, sniffing the air but with purpose now, as if hunting for something of the past. Something lost. Before Ivy could ask him what the matter was, he charged off again, following the scent, high and low, almost frantic in his movements. As the darkness of the passageways came up to meet them, he stopped by an old storeroom door. Scratching at the swollen wood with his worn nails, he turned his head back to Ivy.

"This… In…" he stammered, unable to find the right word with his limited language.

"It's just a storeroom," said Ivy, and she would have smiled or looked quizzically, but in his eyes she saw welling tears of answers that he did not know the questions for. The boy started to try and prize the door from its frame, long sealed by congealed slime in the damp recesses of forgotten castle basements.

"What is it?" Ivy blurted. She could see that he was agitated but she did not understand. Why had he chosen this passageway? What did he know about this door? Could he have…?

"What's in there?" she barked, surprised by her own sound of panic. The boy stopped fingering the door's edge. He did not have the words or the understanding. But he suddenly, vividly, remembered.

"Me," he choked.

She did not know what it meant but she had never seen him behave in this way. He was normally so controlled and purposeful. Yet here could be answers, reasons, explanations to so much that she both wished and did not wish to know. Nevertheless, finally the lock gave way under pressure from a knife she had found in another unlocked room. The ageing green glue suckered away as the reluctant door dislodged from its frame. Creaking, the wooden barrier jolted inwards.

Inside, the room smelt of mould and was icily cold. The panic that had overtaken the boy had gone as the door yielded, trepidation now seeping in. Ivy stood back and watched him enter the darkness, invaded now by the dim candlelight of the corridor. As her eyes grew accustomed to the darkness, she could see his silhouette feeling, sensing the room through touch and smell, crouching and stretching, pausing and flinching. The room itself was relatively bare: an empty storage rack along one wall and an old simple table against the other. Nothing of any note. She could not imagine what affected him in such a way. Still, he traced his hands over the glistening walls, pausing now and again. She knew not to speak, to interrupt his narrative. Then he stopped.

His fingers had found a lose piece of brickwork, and now those calloused tips worked to loosen, prise, shuffle the brick corner loose. Ivy's mind fell on the thought: had he known it was there? Was it by accident, or had he been searching? She stepped towards him, hearing his anxious short breaths in the gloom. As he turned to her, he held a small rolled up piece of parchment between grubby fingers. Carefully, he unrolled the fragment.

"What is it?" Ivy quivered in the dark, but there was no response, the boy now drowning in long-forgotten memory. He turned the paper to Ivy. A short, scrawled message, smudged and blurred. And then a single word.

"Egan," Ivy read, brow furrowed. "Who's Egan?"

The answer fell in a single tear down the boy's cheek.

CHAPTER 13

STONE AND IRON

Fenwood had never felt so vulnerable. The ring of oak which had once seemed so imposing and impenetrable, now appeared frail, permeable, harmless. Rukmahl's ominous words had struck a chord in the heart of the people, who grew steadily frayed by the weakening of their beloved Mother and the uncertainty of the future. They had never faced an enemy before, seen or unseen, and this threat, however distant and unknown, caused doubt and distrust. And in the midst of these ever-widening roots of vulnerability, they clung to the rock of the unshakeable Rukmahl. If he gorged himself on the words and policies of the council, then so would they; he trusted in them, and so would they. It made sense now that wood was weak and that they must begin to rebuild, fortify, solidify. The natural beauty of wood was no match for the security and resolve of iron, such was needed in times of threat. Yet the good, naïve people of Fenwood never once considered that threat could come from within.

Market Day became less about crafts and fancies, increasingly dominated as it now was by masonry and ironwork. Husbands and wives exchanged embroidery and leatherwork for thin sheets of metal, enough perhaps to protect a doorway. Families gave up golden savings for railings. Even flat-iron straps and pokers became noticeable securements on exterior panelled housing. And thus, it began. The people of the city embracing change through fear – their values, traditions, history crumbling and lost through a perception of the wise council. Rukmahl and other elderly council members were seen from time to time in the muddied streets, nodding with approval at these vain attempts. But behind closed doors they knew it needed a more symbolic act.

The sun rose crisp and fine through the morning mist one Market Day. Families began loading their wares for a day of trade and bartering; children guzzled porridge laced with honey and comb; pets trotted to the fireside for their morning stretch. High above the crudely reinforced houses, a single horn pierced the calm. Everyone stopped and turned their eyes skyward as the sound hung with the moisture in the air. It called them.

Rukmahl and the council stood erect on the platform of the beautiful timber hall in the centre of the Market Square, white wispy beards floating in the damp breeze. Rukmahl stifled the grin that threatened to spread across his rubber-jowled face; how ugly this collection of buildings now appeared. How inhospitable. How unnatural. Slowly, tentatively, the people of Fenwood seeped through the mist. Alarmed as they were by the earliness of the hour and the emptiness of the Market Square, the presence of the large, stable figure of Rukmahl brought a sense of ease. He said nothing but waited until it appeared full, then simply nodded whilst stepping aside. A gaunt, pointed man, Councillor Hawkett, lurched forward, emitting a high-pitched squeak as he cleared his throat ready to speak. His beady eyes scanned the crowd like a shrewd scavenger.

"The time has come!" he screeched, an alarming tone that startled and unsettled the vulnerable onlookers. Rukmahl shuffled his bulk forwards and poured whispered words into the ear of the avian speaker. His eyebrows twitched. The gluttonous man at his ear retreated, and when Hawkett spoke again the tone was calmer, as soothing as he could try.

"Good people of Fenwood. You have done much good in preparing for the onslaught"—Rukmahl coughed—"err, difficulties that are surely to come. I and the council are proud of you, for listening and acting so swiftly" —another cough—"and effectively. But we must step up our efforts. There is much to be done to fortify, to secure, and we come with new material."

At this, a muscular figure, clearly unsure of his scripted timing and unfamiliar with public spectacle, stood forth and awkwardly held up a block of stone: shaped, smoothed, dull. "Stone and iron will save you," continued Hawkett. "Stone and iron in place of weak wood." The crowd said nothing. Accepted everything. "And it begins with the Market Hall…"

*   *   *

He had not spoken of it, and she had not asked. They had raced from the grimy underbelly of the castle, the boy gasping for air, gasping for familiarity, gasping for something—anything—natural. He had clattered like a frightened beast through the undergrowth, not waiting for Ivy, not looking back. Emerging days later, he had allowed himself to be found by her, to continue their walks and their conversations. Instinctively, Ivy knew she could not ask, and such was her happiness at being back by his side that she found that the shadow over his personality slid away with the sunlight of his company. So it was that on the day they heard the strange horn blast, it had been drowned out by the blanket of obliviousness that folded itself around them.

They had walked past the Great Crossroads and Ivy had attempted to explain much of the history of Fenwood. The boy had listened to begin with, enthralled, but she soon saw that same expression creep in at the corners of his eyes. Now, as they sat enveloped in the morning mist, she turned to look at him. He was so serene, but a tragedy lay hidden beneath that wild yet calm exterior. The white castle rose in the distance, above the trees, and his gaze searched its ancient towers for… memories? Answers? Almost apologetically she laid her hand on the scuffed skin of his knee, yet he did not recoil. She had to ask.

"Is Egan your name?"

There was a held silence, but it did not become uncomfortable.

"Forest my home," he spoke, without turning to her. "Trees my family." It was the most indirect answer he had ever given and somehow she knew not to press him for more.

"You?" he ventured.

149

"You mean, my family?"

"Yes."

"They've always lived here, in Fenwood."

"Even now?"

"Yes… My mother is the queen. People love her. She is very powerful, and kind, and beautiful. Well, she was…" Something in her last comment, saying it out loud, caught Ivy unawares.

"Was?"

Ivy paused. "Yes. She is sick."

The boy did not know subtlety.

"Why you not look after her?"

"Because… Because…" The fact that she had no answer stung Ivy considerably.

"She die… then you, you be queen?"

Again, no answer.

Within the city walls the first timbers were being torn from the Market Hall.

*   *   *

Ghostly cries and whispered creaks of splitting rafters drifted between the stone frame of the open tower window. They passed through the dreams and nightmares of the frail lady sunken into the sheets of the bed, as deathly pale as the linen. She shivered as sweat beads ran from her forehead and meandered their way across her wrinkled skin. Her lank hair gripped the pillow, her head unable to move for the pain in her skull and the fear that she may stop breathing. She did not even flinch when Ernest entered the room without knocking, and without apology, stumbled to the bedside.

"Mother," he wheezed, "they are tearing down the Market Hall. Our city… Your city… There is metal and, and stone… It is grotesque… A monster…" As he ran out of words his eyes fell upon the Queen's face, unmoving. For a moment he thought her dead. Slowly her skeletal hand rose from the bed, her knotted fingers making no clear gesture.

"Get…" came the croaked voice, "get Mr Rukm—"

"It is HIM!" Ernest interrupted, tears now welling in his eyes. "Him and those damned council men! I told you! I warned you! They have done this! They are tearing apart everything we love, plundering our very lives before our eyes. You must do something, Mother. Must. You…" But as he looked upon her, he saw now how in vain his uncontrolled emotional demands were.

"Ivy…" the Queen croaked. He shook his head.

"No. Not to be found for days. Rumour tells of a friendship with a boy from the outside. She isn't… She…

We should have…" He stopped as the cold, greying hand clasped his shirt cuff.

"Ernest. Find her."

*   *   *

The boy quivered, drew a breath, and squeezed himself through the hanging vines that made a surreptitious door to the boundaries of the city. He could still see Ivy as she meandered her way, conflicted, through the labyrinthine streets. So wrapped up in her own thoughts, she did not notice the gaunt, obtrusive, metallic shapes that made the boy recoil in horror. He stood upright in an attempt to blend in, a camouflage of sorts, but the commotion, the crowds, the sounds and smells were so overwhelming. He collided, ricocheted and balked, losing sight of Ivy who became swallowed up by the panic-stricken crowds. Leaning against a corrugated sheet, the jarring image lost on the bustling crowds, he turned his nose to the air and sniffed. Fear. Molten metal. Otherness.

He had lost her.

*   *   *

Her feet slowly, unconventionally, brought her stuttering

to the doors of the imposing white castle. The stone was coarse to the touch. Creaking, the great door opened, a deathly silence hanging ominously in the stifling air. Ivy's footsteps resounded off the walls, an echoing beat as she ascended the grand, moulded staircase. Following the well-worn corridors, she found herself gazing up at the Queen's tower, spiralling above her. As the steps disappeared behind her, she became more certain that she could hear a voice in the cavernous chambers above. Undoubtably it would be Ernest fawning over Mother… Her mother… And yet the twinge in her stomach had grown into a knot and Ivy's breathing deepened, trying to maintain control. She stepped into the landing area and looked at the door ahead. It had always been 'out of bounds' when she was little, and now it held some secretive power. Her finger traced the lines of the wooden panelling in the door until it came to rest on the handle, cold to the touch. There was resistance to her effort in trying, but it gave under her nervous will.

Her mother lay on the bed, unmoving. A huge bulk hovered above her, dripping in an oversized gown, the source of the whittering words that she had heard from the staircase below. And now the bitterness and anger and poison of those words that belched from the oversized gargoyle came to her ears. The figure did not hear her approach, so engrossed in its own feelings, its own demonic intent. The pillow in its hands covered the Queen's face, pushing down harder. Spittle hung from its teeth and lips. Sweat traversed the bulging features of the face. And when it looked up and saw the girl, it faltered, angry, startled, dangerous. It bared its teeth. The voice, once so powerful it made people drunk with heady euphoria, flashed with brutality.

"How dare you interrupt ME!" Rukmahl threw the pillow away. He began to haul his slug-like frame around the bed. Ivy was frozen, detached from emotion.

"Well, if this isn't the damned Gods speaking" – a tongue flickered at the corner of his mouth – "a chance to wipe out the bitch and the pup." He drew up to his full height, towering over the girl. She began to crumble.

Rukmahl raised his hand above his head and brought the back of his fingers and knuckles crashing down onto the soft flesh of Ivy's cheek, the gaudy rings smashing the bone. Her body hit the cold, hard floor with the thud of dead weight. Fiendishly, lasciviously, he straddled his immense mass over her and began pawing at her clothes; a sneer remained etched into his clay face, glistening with joyful exertion. As his hands closed around her throat, so intense was his obsession that he did not see the attack springing from the doorway. Shoulder and forearm struck

Rukmahl's jaw beneath folds of fat, knocking him back, sending him sprawling on the flagstones. His attacker wasted no time in pouncing again, instinctively nullifying its prey with limbs pinning Rukmahl to the ground. The boy sat glaring at the figure beneath him, controlled aggression in his eyes, and then jolted his view to Ivy. She was motionless, but the rise and fall of her breast told him that life flowed through her. His head flicked round to see the woman on the bed. Unmoving. He sniffed the air. Deathly still. She meant nothing to him but he sensed she was important. From the doorway the wail of an old man startled the boy and he turned to see a sobbing, white-haired man dropping to his knees.

*   *   *

In the days that followed, Fenwood existed in a stunned silence. Work slowed. Trade stuttered. Conversations dried up in open mouths. The people were shocked, horrified, embarrassed, guilty, vulnerable. Partly they were appalled that their idyllic, simple life had been ripped apart by murder and corruption, but there was also a deeper, sickening knowledge that, underneath it all, they had known. How many times had they wondered about his potions? How many had let his grotesque, chubby hands slide over their bodies? How many had spoken their darkest suspicions aloud? They had not played any role in the final act, but they had turned a blind eye in the scenes of Rukmahl's devastating tragedy. And whilst they hid that guilt behind wide-eyed condemnation, the weight of the culpability crushed their spirit.

'The boy' became the conversation outlet. There had been rumoured whispers of a 'distraction', something that was keeping Ivy from her commitments, from her inevitable future. From the moment they had been led down from the tower, Egan had clung to Ivy, not through his own fear but his primal instinct to protect her. Oblivious to the stares, he had wrapped his arms around her as she clung to him, holding her as she stumbled over the uneven stone steps, somehow finding every crack, divot, moss-slick. But once safe, he had begun to feel eyes on him. A scrutiny of his movements and mannerisms that were so far removed from Ivy's idealisation. They had tried to talk to him, some even to touch him, and his natural recoil surprised them into giggles, like the behaviour of a beloved pet. It made him uncomfortable, desiring to run back to the freedom of the forest. Yet he could not leave her.

*   *   *

Such was the outrage and condemnation, Rukmahl's trial was a mere formality; a performance staged as an opportunity to gawp and sneer and shout profanity. He had offended not only the people and the land, but the Gods themselves, so the folk of Fenwood said. He stood in the centre of the Market Place, a cold stare in his eyes and a demonic curling at the edge of his lips. The elders, dressed in gaudy ceremonial gowns, could barely be heard above the din of the crowd as they declared his crimes and proclaimed his guilt. Only the history books could speak of the last time someone had been put to death as punishment for their crimes, but the thirsty crowd bellowed their approval at the announcement for Rukmahl. The betrayer. The murderer.

Stood upon the dais, tears fell from Ivy's eyes and, body remaining stonelike, she searched for Egan in the ever-baying mob. She could not see him. Maybe he had hidden away from this furore, this spectacle, and she could not blame him. Instead, her eyes met those of her attacker across the open space, and the noise around her fell to a faraway din. His face bore the red marks and bruises of torture, but the fire of life and defiance still roared in his eyes. A rock, launched from the watching mass, struck Rukmahl on the back and he reeled forward onto his knees, forced into a position of begging. But looking up and meeting Ivy's eyes once again, he spat in her direction. Instantly the Chief of the Guard, Tindal, yanked him backwards and dragged him, stumbling, back through the guard-lined avenue towards the castle dungeon. Ivy closed her eyes and allowed the tears to fall freely. They were not tears for her mother, and certainly not for Rukmahl, but for herself. She was not ready for what would come next.

CHAPTER 14

DEATH OF A TRAITOR

Just as they had done for his first appearance at his market stall, most of Fenwood rolled out for Rukmahl's final appearance, though now with utter contempt and hatred rather than wonder and adulation. The cries of, "Help me" and, "Praise him" were replaced by, "Murderer!" and, "Burn him!" Fenwood had always been a city of peace and harmony; its good people now united in anger and bloodlust.

In centuries gone by, the Great Crossroads had served as a place of execution; bodies were strung up in crow cages on the merchant way as a deterrent to wrong-doers. Perhaps it had worked, or perhaps those people realised that there was no gain in crime in such a reclusive area, but the last execution had long passed out of living memory. Indeed, many of Fenwood's more knowledgeable (or nosy) inhabitants took to the record books in the days before Rukmahl's trial. Yet on the day of the execution, the history of such an event went unmentioned, and all sense of tradition or ordered ceremony was lost beneath seething rage and heart-felt outcries.

The diminished figure was dragged up Fenwood Road, chained to four guards who had walked at a pace alien to the guilty man. His bare feet bled from the stones in the path, his wrists worn with lacerations made by the iron cuffs. The exquisite clothes had been torn from the man's body and in their place hung white sack-cloth garments, already stained with sweat and dirt and blood. Whilst the bulk of his figure was still evident beneath the shapeless cloth, the fat that had once sat pompously as a sign of luxury and indulgence now hung and sagged; a once proud beast long since past its prime, left to wallow in warped reminiscence and growing disdain. Perhaps most shocking was his face: shaven, roughly, from scalp to chin. Gone were the proud locks that hung at his shoulders and the meticulously trimmed beard. His tresses had clearly been cut with a knife blade, leaving small chunks of hair and shallow wounds that seeped across the baldness of the scalp. But more than this, Rukmahl had changed. He whimpered. He cowered. He muttered to himself. The Rukmahl who had charged into the small city of Fenwood appeared utterly bereft and destroyed.

On one corner of the crossroads a circle of stones had been lain down, the width of two men. In the centre, a pyre had been carefully built; an orderly construct, with three different woods interwoven in a stack. On the top, quite securely, lay a large board onto which Rukmahl would be taken and tied to the birch stake around which the wooden scaffold had been made. Even as Rukmahl was dragged through his final steps, between the crowds of onlookers, some collected up sticks, shards of bark and other kindling to throw at the base of the pyre. This way they could say that they had played their part. Despite his evident decline, the once great man never lowered his eyes to the floor and seemed to hold the glares of the good people he had wronged. The crowd murmured and angered. Restraint showed on their faces as he passed them by, tripping and shuffling on the gravel. By now the crowd had fallen into silence, listening to the chink of the chains and the shifting of the guards' armour as they marched.

As Rukmahl passed Hops, nearing the stone circle, he fell. No attempt was made from the crowd to help. On Hops' face passed a look of resentment and false trust; the result of an excess of wine, meat and stories that had been shared by the fireside, now all a lie. The innkeeper rolled his chewing tobacco around his mouth and spat it at the man who had abused his trust and confidence, hitting Rukmahl below the left eye. When Rukmahl was hoisted to his feet, the two men looked at each other. No words were exchanged, but Hops' mind flooded with everything he wanted to say. Rukmahl held the gaze and Hops' eyes dropped to his feet.

Time lingered as the guilty man passed through the crowd, each moment filled with such emotion and memory. As Rukmahl was led up to the pyre, each person could recall exactly where they were when they had first met the traitor, and what he had said. Now, standing guarded on the platform, his eyes fell upon them all. Stepping forward, the Chief of the Guard cleared his throat.

"This man is brought before you charged and convicted of high treason. Here his body shall be burnt and left as a reminder of the price that is paid for such a crime against the Gods, our queen and her people."

At this he wiped his brow of sweat and let out a sigh. Struggling for words, he allowed his formal tone to drop.

"A sad day is this. It is long since we have suffered such at the hands of an traitor – today we must reopen a bloody chapter in Fenwood's history." Turning to Rukmahl, his voice full of disappointment rather than malice, he continued. "I have spoken with you many times, sir. I understand these people's anger and hatred, and yet from me there is sadness and pity. Many people have been cured here at your hand, and yet you do us the ultimate sickness in this act. I hope your last words will be of remorse."

A silence followed, the intention being for Rukmahl to speak, but no words were offered.

"You have nothing to say?" uttered Chief Tindal, with weight in his trailing voice. But the response came back clear and assured, as of old.

"I have much to say, my dear chief, and much that cannot be said. I am shocked and delighted that the folk of this peace-loving place would bestow upon me the honour of a final audience." Suddenly the people hung on his every word. "You have been wronged. You have been misled. You deserve repentance and remorse." A pause. "But I will not give it to you." And a change came into Rukmahl's voice; a tremor of an almost mystical malice. "For all your pitiful traditions and pathetic ceremonies to preserve the goodliness and godliness of what you have, you are missing a universal truth: time moves on. The world outside of your hallowed Oaken Ring mocks you and plots to destroy you. I came here to save you from an apocalyptic fate, and I will proclaim it from my throne of fire. A time is coming when you will all suffer through torture and violence and bloodshed; and I will look upon you, and I will laugh."

The voice echoed through the trees, piercing every silence, surrounding the people of Fenwood; a terrified congregation to a demonic preacher.

As the echo faded, the spell seemed to break. The City Guard dragged Rukmahl to the stake and the crowd once again became audible; the hatred intensified by the parting words. The pariah was yanked back to the birch stake, forcibly enough that his head whipped with a loud crack against the hard wood. The pain never registered on his face, nor was there even a flicker of emotion as thick rope was wound around him, pulled tight with each coil so that it burnt against his skin through the white cloth. And then it was done. Bound beyond escape at the centre of the great pyre, the symbol of hatred and evil, of weakness and gullibility, was detained, controlled, and soon to be extinguished.

The expectant crowd lulled to a sinister hush. The torch had been lit and the Chief of the Guard carried the flaming brand with an air of ceremony, hoping to maintain a sense of order to the proceedings. Not once did he look up at the trapped beast, tied with rope that drew blood to the surface. He stopped only for a moment before the base of sticks and kindling. With a final sigh, he plunged the torch into the midst of the natural debris. The twigs, branches and bark took the flame quickly, welcoming their moment to cleanse the town of impurity. Soon the arms of the fire were grasping at the wooden board of the pyre, smoke billowing so that Rukmahl was hidden from view. Many people craned their necks, waiting to glimpse the moment when the traitor felt the wrath of the flame. This moment remained masked from them, but a gut-wrenching howl rose from the centre of the burning mass. The fire had found its target.

As it burned ever higher, the smoke floated upwards, clearing the view. Some gasped, others kept an insistent expression, but many were forced to look away. Had the flames revealed Rukmahl to be a God of the Deepfires, it would perhaps have been less of a shock to the inhabitants of Fenwood. Yet the traitor was clearly flesh and bone. The white cloth fizzed away and turned to ash, raining down upon the crowd. Then the flaming hands grasped at Rukmahl's skin, smoking it, scorching it, and eventually melting it away from the body. The stench of burning flesh crept mercilessly over the steadily sickening crowd; a chorus of choking and retching joined the tumultuous roar of the fire.

The sight became more violent, brutal beyond expectation. Those who had brought children to the reckoning hastily led them away amidst their tears and sobs, followed by others who could no longer stand to watch the destruction.

All the while, Rukmahl continued to howl maniacally with excruciating pain. His outer layer of skin had all but burnt away, and with the intensity of the fire and heat, his flesh had begun to catch alight. He became a scorched black mass, somewhat less human and more skeletal as the flesh cooked, shrivelled and deteriorated amongst the flames. Yet he remained alive, against all laws of nature. The heart still beat, the eyes still moved, and the body strained. The rope had long been devoured by the fire and the traitor's body melted onto the central wooden column as the flesh boiled. The crowd became increasingly horrified with each moment and lick of flames that passed. When Farmer Stenson had been trapped in a burning barn five years previous, his heart had given up to the pain well before the fire has attacked his body. They stared in disbelief at the roaring, vulgar figure in front of them; a traitor not only to them and their queen, but seemingly to humanity. His final words ringing in their ears, they listened to his chorus of anguish bellowing from the throne of fire.

And then the rains came. Without warning, a crash of thunder and a blanket of water issued from above. The City Guards strove to laden the pyre with yet more kindling to maintain the fire, but the rain began to subdue the flaming mass. As the water fell onto the scorched, flailing remains of the once great man at the centre, an uncomfortable hissing sound ensued, and thin tendrils of steam snaked away from the charred body. Rukmahl continued to howl, words destroyed by incredible suffering but life still evident in the burnt and blackened skeleton. The remaining crowd, a dwindling, sickened few, stood dumbstruck, but still held their almost demonic vigil.

The quiet that descended as Rukmahl's cries subsided only proved the violence of the scene that had preceded it. It was not a silence, as a hiss continued to drift on the wind, interjected with coughs and splutters from the charcoaled man. The rage of Fenwood had been burnt away by brutality leaving a sour and horrified residue. And Rukmahl was, unbelievably, still alive.

Chief Tindal broke his gaze from the pyre. Surveying the depleted crowd, he saw the same horror and shame in the eyes of the few remaining men that he felt flowing through his own body. Quickly, he drew his ceremonial sword from its gilded scabbard and ascended the smoking pyre. At last, he made eye contact with the villain, looking into the whites that penetrated from the darkness. In those moments he read less humanity and remorse than before; just glazed, emotionless pools. Placing his hand on the flaking, scorched forehead, he tilted the head back, exposing the throat. With one hefty swing, the cold steel blade struck the jugular and sliced clean through, wedging the sword blade into the wooden pole behind. For a moment the head stared back at Tindal, taunting him. No blood fell from the neck as finally the head toppled from the shoulders, landing on the platform with a thud amongst the embers; expressionless.

Fire burns. Destroys.

    Water cleanses. Restores

    Nature dies. Is reborn.

    Death is necessary.

    Ivy.

    Ivy.

CHAPTER 15

LAURENT'S TASK

The pyre remained untouched for some time. No one came to clear it, check or even look at the ghostly debris of destruction, like a guilty secret, a reminder of their bloody lust. Rukmahl had been such a commanding figure in life, bringing assurance and mislaid reliability, that even now in disgraced death, his influence hung in darkened shadows over the cowering city of Fenwood. His bottles adorned people's shelves, his shop remained untouched. His letters, pamphlets and advice hurriedly packed away from folks' tables. He was a memory, a legacy, a stain. And yet, reviled as he now was, Fenwood froze in terror. They did not trust the council. They did not trust each other.

Tindal held the flaming torch carefully in front of him,

away from hanging branches, so the firelight parted the imposing darkness. He knew he was getting closer from the intensifying stench, the unmistakable smell of decaying death. And yet, as putrid as the smell was, it could not prepare him for the sight that confronted him. Enclosed within the stone circle the chaos contrasted savagely with the surrounding landscape. Rukmahl's headless body now hung away from the charred stake, attached still by one arm with the other dangling to the side, severed below the shoulder. Across the body, the skin, or what remained if it, had turned grey with rot. It was patchy, having been burnt or torn from the bones by carrion birds.

"A fitting end, you poison," was all the guard could manage to say. Not touching the carcass, Tindal began to dig a hole at the base of the central wooden pillar, large enough for the burial of a corpse. When ready, he merely swung his sword at the remaining arm and the ragged skeleton tumbled into the awaiting pit. Bones fell to the sides and Tindal kicked them unceremoniously into the heap. As he covered the remains with the dug soil, he thought about saying a few words but rejected the notion. He never had been much of a talker.

"I am sorry for you. You could have done good here. But you do not deserve any service," and continued shovelling. In days to come, when townsfolk drifted back to the pyre through intrigue and found the body gone, they assumed the anti-gods had come to claim back one of their own. Little did they realise he lay in pieces beneath their feet, reclaimed by nature.

Ivy had stayed in her mother's chamber from the moment that the Queen had been buried. The outpouring of grief at the public ceremony had been a torrent of emotion: sobbing, wailing, collapsing. Ivy had remained stoic, unflinching, unwavering. A sign of strength, perhaps? They hoped. A sign that she would adopt her mother's position with regality and reverence? They dreamed. Days drifted by and a hope that Ivy was preparing for a great public address gathered among the people. Eyes peered up at the towers and windows, praying for a sign, a calling. But nothing came. They did not know that the girl on whom their future rested stood behind the veiled net curtain of the highest tower window, and whilst she stood and gazed over the lands, her heart still yearned for the forests beyond.

The boy became Egan. Thrust into the public eye, he became a civilised version of himself. Coached to stand up straight, dressed in embroidered silks, bewildered by etiquette and enunciation. He was a welcome sight on the winding streets of Fenwood, smiling and full of wonder. The layers of tradition and decorum had not been weighted on him, so he felt like a fresh breeze of hope to the crushed inhabitants. Ivy watched him with intrigue. Her joy at seeing him seemingly embrace his new life was tinged with sadness that she now had to share him, and in these alien surroundings. He showed no signs of discomfort or regret, but the memory of the subterranean castle corridor crawled back to her. There was so much of him that was unknown, hidden beneath layers of wilderness and solitude. He enjoyed being with people, but he was not one of them; an amusing sideshow at the fair of despair.

Egan sat on the castle steps, giggling to himself as he cracked pistachios from their shells. He admired the green of the nut within before popping them into his mouth and throwing the shell at a nearby gutter-hole. Suddenly he felt the hairs on his neck stand alive and he leapt up and turned in one swift movement. Laurent stood in the doorway, the light from the flaming torch casting his angular shadow against the white castle wall. Egan closed his lips over his bared teeth. Laurent's head was sunken forward, his shoulders high. They passed an awkward, complex moment. The grotesque servant broke the silence.

"She does not love you," he sneered. Egan understood the words but not the intent. He held the strength of his unblinking gaze on Laurent.

"You go back to castle," Egan growled, not as a threat but stern advice. Laurent smiled, attempting to mask the fear in his eyes. Egan had already seen it and took a step toward him. Laurent recoiled. "You, weak man," Egan pressed, sensing an easy victory, his assured steps forward forcing the vulnerable carer into the doorway behind. Laurent's head hit the hanging arch and he cowered below the figure of the once-forest boy, now an imposing man rearing over him. Sensing the weakness of his prey, Egan dropped his shoulders and returned to a semi-hunch. He waited a moment, inspecting Laurent sprawled on the floor in front of him. Feeling no threat, he turned leaving the defeated servant holding back angry tears.

*   *   *

Beneath the sign of the Oak and Maize, Hops' inn became a place of solace; a meeting place that, unlike the Market Square, had no link with recent traumatic events. Its rustic, wooden tables gathered together those in need of company, in need of distraction or, indeed, those in need of drowning their own sadness and guilt. Within the simple décor and by the crackling fire, one could find what one needed. Whilst he could not deny that more patrons were good for his business, Hops had never truly embraced the inn as a means of becoming successful. In those difficult days, he marvelled that such wanton hate had brought the public house to its true identity: community. He was a man of simple needs and pleasures, and finally he was bringing people together and providing comfort. He moved between the rows of people, a contented invisible figure providing food and beverages. He wished them, "Gods give you good night," as the gatherers dispersed, before locking the door and securing the carved inn sign; reminders that he was helping in the way the Gods intended.

The sun sank in gloom on yet another day, the people's hearts and hopes fading with it. Secretly, hidden from view, Ivy watched them go. She longed to give them comfort, order, security, but she could not be who they wanted her to be. Ruefully she let out a sigh, an expression of sadness and frustration. She had anguished over what decisions to make for the people... her people. But that truth seemed altogether alien to her. The truth was that she did not know what to do. She was not her mother. And with that reality solidly in mind, Ivy pulled her deerskin coat from the recess in the ancient stone wall and slid her arms through, adjusting it over her shoulders before heading to the doorway. She was careful not to tread in the middle of the walkways in case the creaks and murmurs of the ageing wooden planks gave away her retreat. Shadows clung to every wall, cloaking her. Colours of dusk grew up the interior stone, and as she stepped off the final stair, Ivy looked up through a window above her to witness the moon awakening to welcome the coming night. The entrance hall felt desolate as the young princess crossed between the shafts of moonlight and, hardly opening the door a fraction, she slipped through and out into the growing, shielding night.

A shadow in the hallway moved. A grotesque, angular outline crept along the wall. It caught the door before it shut and slunk out behind the maiden.

*   *   *

Seated around the gilded, polished table, the eyes of the old, crooked faces peered intently at the withered man-child that sprawled awkwardly in the chair. Even though the table was round, everything seemed to face him. He wriggled and writhed, trying to avoid their words; frightened, anxious, confused.

"Laurent," came a deep almost soothing voice from the indistinct murmurs. "You know what we say is true. With the queen gone, Ivy should be leading her people from the anguish. But she is faltering and failing the good people of this once great to…err, city." He glanced, unnoticed by the servant, at the faces around him with a smile of growing confidence. "You spent such time with her, helping prepare her for this inevitable moment. But… but now she has betrayed you and your friendship."

This word stung Laurent into looking up, and the wrinkled face of the councilman saw his moment.

"Yes. Yes, she betrayed your loyalty to her. And to this city." He could see in the weakling's eyes that the words were taking hold. "If there is anyone who can bring her back, it is you. Her great friend. Her true friend. Not this, this… leaf-green upstart…"

Laurent hissed, "A coward."

"Yes!" cried several members of the council. Laurent felt the embers of self-importance ignite inside him. The deep voice opposite spoke up again.

"Laurent. Look at me. We need you. This city needs you. She needs you." A gulp from the angular shape in the chair. "We know that you have *always* been underestimated by the people… everyone. They don't know your strength—"

"I could show them!" Laurent interrupted.

"Yes, yes! It is so important that you find her. Confront her. Make her see the truth."

A silence fell, but the atmosphere in the room had

changed. Laurent sat upright, eyes bright. He looked around the circle of wizened faces, feeling power, feeling control, vulnerably unaware of the strings they had him puppeted on. He wondered what they were waiting for.

"Well?" he said, unwittingly closing the trap. "What can I do to help?"

The plan was all too easy for him. Yes, he knew she was leaving the castle at night. Yes, he knew she met with the forest boy. He watched. He watched each movement, each secret expression, each thought. He knew her. And he would make her see what was needed, what was right.

"And should she need further persuasion," sidled in the crooked man with the flickering eyelid, "this might help." A firm grip of swollen joints took Laurent's wrist with surprising power, pulling it forward, and into his hand was placed an object; a wooden handle and metal shaft with a small protruding catch teasingly alongside the forefinger. Laurent had never seen anything like it. He looked up quizzically.

"It's a form of weapon, hugely popular in the Western lands. Pull that lever and it makes quite the noise. Terrify her. She'll come to our way of thinking in no time."

"This lever?" Laurent innocently asked, repositioning his finger.

"Don't!" came the immediate cry from several bearded

mouths.

"Yes," came the calmer, considered response from the giver of the weapon. "But wait until you are near them, it will trigger such a reaction." Laurent stood and slid the item, cold, into his jacket pocket. All eyes were on him. In them he saw understanding and confidence.

"Go do this great deed. Make them see yours, and Fenwood's, strength."

Laurent nodded and went from the room, dragging his foot slightly behind him. The door closed. Silence. The silence of expectant success.

*   *   *

The branches lowered noiselessly as his hands carefully parted them. He had followed her silhouette silently through the brush, so he was wary of not startling them now. Ahead, in a secluded clearing illuminated by the waxing moon, Ivy sat in enraptured conversation with the wild boy, although Laurent noted that he wore some sort of flannel shirt over his body. He was not talking, but gazed intently at the girl. In voyeuristic obsession, Laurent experienced a sense of sadness; jealousy and anger bubbled inside. Why was he no longer the one she wanted to talk to, to share with? Yes, he may be ugly to look at, but he was refined and intelligent, and human. Not some beast. Some freak. He tried to control his breathing, calm himself. And then he stopped breathing altogether. In front of him, glimmering in the soft night light, the boy placed his hand over hers; exploratively, deliberately. Instantly she stopped talking. Surely she would recoil? Straining to see more, Laurent clutched the branch and convinced himself that she was disgusted. But, leaning in, Ivy looked from Egan's eyes to his lips, finally giving in to her fascination. The boy closed his eyes to accept the softness of her lips on hers. Lost in each other, they did not hear the savage crack of a breaking branch. Laurent saw them in slowed time. The frustration that had long been held latent became overwhelmed by visceral loathing. Teeth gritted, tears of anger welling in his eyes, he looked frantically for something to destroy his nightmare. No stones. No boughs. But the coldness of the weapon tucked to his back screamed at him. Clasping it in his good hand, he raised the muzzle in front of him, the scene blurred by flowing tears.

Boom.

At the sound of the shot they didn't look back but ran, crashing through the woodland. Egan lost Ivy's hand as trees parted them, roots pushing their paths apart. He was aware that she was screaming and racing without thought, tearing her dress as she disappeared into the enveloping forest. He turned towards her direction, but another roaring explosion quickly followed by something passing by his ear made him duck to the ground. Picking himself up he fled, feet feeling once again the ebb and flow of the woodland floor, hands easing his passing through the trees.

Ivy screamed uncontrollably. Her white dress was ragged in places, torn and stained by the wooded maze that thrashed and beat against her skin. She dared not look back, dared not look for Egan. She tripped and stumbled over the ground that seemed to move and slide beneath her. Her chest hurt. Her head hurt. But she kept running. And a second boom somewhere behind her dragged another scream from her lips.

Egan burst through the undergrowth onto the mudded path. Pausing to look around, he could see the Great Crossroads to his left. Would Ivy head there?

Ivy burst through the treeline, movement blocked by a hedgerow. Ahead of her a field of golden wheat swayed heavily in the growing wind. She knew where she was. If she could only get to the pool.

Laurent saw the figure ahead of him stop. His arm

raised. Blinded by besotted hatred.

Click.

Boom.

The body dropped to the floor.

CHAPTER 16

THE POOL

The rustling of trees in the wind. The call of wild animals. Danger! Danger! The gathering of grey clouds, slowly pushing away fragments of blue sky. A body lying at the centre of the crossroads; clothes that had sat so uncomfortably now seeping in mud, staining the regal colours. Mud matted the hair to the forehead, slickened by beads of sweat that had long formed on the brow but were now disappearing as the body grew colder. The face was vacant as though concentrating on some far away task. But the figure did not move, and the woodland held its breath…

Ivy

Ivy

Ivy

"Ivy," whispered Egan.

The eyes opened. The body lurched upwards with a renewed purpose and became once again Egan. He searched his stained body with his hands, picking off congealed lumps of mud as he did so, feeling life flowing back through his limbs. There was no wound. He had not been shot. But then who…?

"Ivy," he whispered again.

Egan ran.

The arms of the trees did not hinder him as he raced in the direction in which he had heard the noise of the instrument of death; rather the trees pushed at his back and the wind hurried him on, anxious for him to reach the princess before it was too late. He became tired quickly, the weight of the mud in his clothes slowed him and he struggled to free himself of his outer robe, leaving it trailing in his wake as he managed to heave it from his wrists. Yet it was not enough, all his garments were heavy with mud.

Ivy.

As best he could, Egan tore at his clothes as he ran, leaving behind him a trail of finest cloth. His body received the touch of the trees and leaves onto his naked skin as a caress, a loving embrace, until all that remained was his loincloth, with his flesh revealed to nature for the first time since… He paused…

Ivy.

And on he ran. The woodland became denser and the young man was forced to duck and weave between trunks and branches, often dropping to his haunches; hands and knuckles on the ground assisting his feet to spring over natural debris on the woodland floor.

Ivy.

His eyes became desperate, wide and frenzied, green light piercing the undergrowth. His pace quickened, cutting his knuckles on the ground as they pounded on fallen foliage, turning it as he blundered on. Branches marked his skin, leaving whip marks of black, green, brown, and, occasionally, blood red.

He had long passed the farmhouse and paddocks when he halted suddenly, surveying the air, before turning sharp left down the hill. The mud slipped and slid beneath his bare feet, unable to provide the boy with a grip on the forest base and his hands clawed at the rocks to spur him on, frantic.

Ivy.

She was close. Or had to be. A field opened up to his right; a vast expanse of wheat intermittently disrupted by sharp blasts of colour as poppies sprung between the stalks. On his left was the hedgerow, but he knew what lay beyond. The wood boy ran on, desperately looking left and…

Ivy.

White cloth floating in the breeze, just visible above the cropped wheat.

Ivy.

Silken hair wrapped around the golden stalks.

Ivy.

Blood. Red on white. The beautiful white dress, hand embroidered by the women of Fenwood, tainted by blood red death. Ivy's skin was as cold and white as her fine garb. He stroked her cheek and wiped the final tears that she had cried in pain. And he leaned over and kissed her.

Ivy.

*　　　　*　　　　*

It seemed like hours, but seconds later he looked up. The wind rattled through the trees and across the field, picking up loose leaves, burrs, petals and grains, catching them up in its whistling arms and casting them into the sky, as if Nature and the Gods wept for the girl. Yet as it did so, it played across the surface of the pool, awakening it with the sound of twinkling bells. The boy heard the music and, scooping the princess into his arms, he pushed through the hedgerow. The trees saw him coming and opened their boughs to him like a great curtain. The music trailed away, and the final limbs of ash and elm parted. The children had arrived.

The pool was alive. It cast off its dormant years, renewing its splendour from the time of the Gods. The trees still guarded the water but now stood erect and dutiful like kings of old. The water shimmered in the drowsy sun, casting more light than should have been reflected, but was ever still.

The boy stepped forward. The girl lay lifeless in his arms. The trees dropped and bowed to him; he was welcome. He was expected. With the girl clenched close to his body, he took another step towards the water's edge. He hesitated for a moment, and then penetrated the unbroken surface of the water.

The tails of Ivy's dress caught the water and floated in the ripples that the boy's body made as he strode through the pool, parting the lilies. Soon the water was to his waist. He glanced down at the girl in his arms, unaware that tears were falling down his cheeks until he had to blink them from his eyes to see clearly. She was pale. Too pale. White skin blended to white cotton, now stained mercilessly with blood that soaked the fibres and spread. When the water covered his arms and edged its way up Ivy's body, he stopped. The air seemed not to move as the trees held their breath, arms frozen over the pool. The boy moved his lips as if to speak, but no sound was heard, no words could be found. He listened for the music that had drawn him to this place, but it had stopped. The girl was dead. He was too late.

Slowly he raised her head up, her arms falling limp to her sides,hitting the water; all colour drained from her body, pale under the wet, clinging dress. His tears fell freely now onto her face; her closed eyes, her parted lips.

"Ivy," he whispered, and kissed her. Carefully he lowered his arms back to the water and, still watching her, allowed the pool to seep up over the sides of her body until the vision of beauty became a mirage under the motion of the water. The great boughs of the trees, now stooped through sickness to the water, felt the disturbance; not just in the tension of the surface, but in a magic time had long since forgotten. Gently the brittle and liver-spotted branches caressed the small waves back towards the beings that had penetrated the peace and oblivious tranquillity.

The boy stood motionless, dumbstruck. Somewhere his mind was forming the question, "Why did I come here?"

But all he could do was look down through the water at the lifeless body of the girl he loved, unable to let go and give her to the pool. Small hands under the surface had taken hold of Ivy's garments and the muddied figure could feel her being pulled away. He clenched his fingers into the remaining grip that he had, but those watery hands soothed his bruised and bloodied knuckles with a softness that spoke to him.

"We will look after her. She is safe."

And slowly he loosened his grip.

*   *   *

Laurent tore through the brush, nature's whipping pain of plants and branches not registering through his blind panic. He had heard the rapid movement of a beast hurtling through the undergrowth. Too big to be a woodland animal. What? The boy? Then who had…? Water fell from his eyes, smudging the tree stains across his cheeks. His hands flapped in front of him, still clutching the metal source of his madness, swatting at branches as his lumbering body crashed through the wild land, a constant obstacle to his search. At last, a trodden path, and in the near distance the glint of light off water. Laurent, half crazed, skidded on the dusty shingle as the path fell away revealing the edge of a pool, so still in his now chaotic world. In time gone by a stone staircase had been layered into the short incline, some of which remained; Laurent took each step with a half stumble, half jump until he was at the water's edge, at the back of the pool, his view somewhat hampered by huge boughs of stately trees. Beneath two of these arms a ramshackle wooden bridge had been positioned with a definite path on the other bank. Not checking his footing, Laurent lunged onto the bridge, creaking under his ungainly stature and shaking as he reached the middle. And then he stopped.

In the centre of the pool Laurent could see a figure, darkened by the glints of light off the water that surrounded it. As the serving boy squinted, he could see the being was wild in appearance, greened by the hue of the natural world around him, and yet in keeping with it. In his arms, just beneath the calm surface of the water, he relinquished a body.

A body.

A female body.

A female.

Laurent's anguished cry was piercing, full of heartbreak and terror, but incidental; a personal torment in a greater devastation. His knees buckled and his gnarled hands grasped at the rotting wood of the bridge rail. The weapon in his hand fell from his grip and, almost without a sound, was engulfed by the pool, lost within the reeds. The boy on the bridge collapsed to his knees, a crumpled wreck, a mass of tortured body and scarred visage, wracked with tears.

Ivy's body drifted beneath the water; her beloved Egan was unmoving, undistracted, tears falling heavily onto the surface of the water. Finally, his eyelids could stand the stinging no longer and they closed.

Ivy.

*   *   *

A blinding light. Egan screwed his eyes tighter and was drawn from his solace to shield his face. On the bridge, the crumpled heap drew a cloak over itself. The wind stirred in the trees, whistling through and creaking the branches, skimming down across the surface of the water and surrounding the figure at its centre. The sound of the trees and the wind and the water combined into a cacophony of noise that encircled and trapped the standing boy, pulling at his cheeks. The din hung at his ears, blocking any thought and becoming as painful as the sheer light on his eyes. And then a single voice singing through, quietening all: "Egan."

The eyes flickered open, searching through the light for the source of the harmonic voice. A girl, with full, deep brown hair and clear green eyes drifted through the water towards him. The pool did not part but offered no resistance in her movement toward him, smoothly, with her arms outstretched. Egan, unable to move, felt his hands being taken from his side and raised. He knew the face, the figure, the voice, but he did not understand. And then he felt the warm, comforting embrace.

"Do not be afraid. I am here."

CHAPTER 17

FALLING STONE

The metallic crashes from the forest were the stones that released the avalanche. The trussed-up anxiety, the threat of invasion, the fraught tension all set loose in a single driven moment of pain and hatred. The vulnerability of those poor, simple folk flooded out in screaming chaos and mayhem into the convoluted streets of Fenwood. Men and women and children weeping, wailing, purposeless, leaderless, abandoning houses and all sense of control. They knew not where to turn, who to turn to. Frantic realisation that their demise was nearing overtook them. Houses were packed up and raided. Friends both comforted each other and fought. Businesses were closed up and demolished. Disarray. Chaos. Hops offered the space at his inn for solace, but was soon overrun. Never had the city seen, or even imagined, such utter despair.

*   *   *

Laurent regained consciousness with a savage intake of breath. His buckled body lurched forwards from the shoulders, breaking the natural peace that had settled over the pool and bough-protected clearing. He looked furtively this way and that, trying to make sense of what he had done, what he had seen. Chaos reigned over his mind.

Ivy.

He had… Again, his body reeled forwards but this time his throat wrenched with stinging bile that emptied from his mouth, splattering the bridge slats beneath his body. Gripping the railing he hauled his numb form to its knees, wheezing, breathing erratic. Spontaneous sobs broke through intermittently.

Ivy.

In his mind's eye he saw her… Radiant smile that sparkled in sea green eyes… Playful teasing and innocent flirtations… White dress billowing over the yellows and greens of Fenwood fields… White cotton… stained with blood… He hauled his disfigured frame along the bridge, desperate to flee from the self that had committed the heinous sin. Guilt clung to him like water weeds, dragging him back.

Reaching the bank on the far side, Laurent scrambled up the stone verge to a path. It swung left through the trees, winding through the forest to join the thoroughfare to the main gateway set in the Oaken Ring. Looking right, Laurent's way was blockaded by briars and dense unknown. Echoes of the mechanical explosion and screams rushed up from the pool behind him, reverberating in his head. He retched again, the guilt twisting his stomach and stretching his guts. Hands outstretched, blindly fleeing his crime, the tormented puppet turned right and crashed through the undergrowth.

*　　　　　*　　　　　*

For some time, the decrepit men of the council hid away in their grand rooms, either afraid or unsure of how to deal with the mass hysteria below. They looked out from the shadows of arched windows, cowering from the wails of despair that crawled up the towers to grasp them.

"They will blame us! Tear us apart!" cried out Blastington, leaning across the table as yet another meeting descended into acrimony.

"They already do," came the barbed reply.

"At least if we go down to them, we can be perceived as empathising, feeling their suffering…"

And so it was, three days after the sound of violence from the forest, that the men from the council came into the city, came to give assurance, but out of touch and past time. For the city they stepped into, resembling a post-apocalyptic war-torn setting, had grieved and were now asking questions. What? Why? Who? And with their beards of pompous arrogance, their garb of alienated superiority, the twelve men cast themselves as the villains, the answers, the startling realisation of truth for the people. Through the dust they padded, vision blurred by clouded air and false safety; more and more red, swollen eyes turned to look on them with hatred and blame. The awkward silence the council initially took as pain became a growing, ominous threat.

The decision was made to spread out in order to cover the city and speak to its people; it was not unanimous, but nevertheless those deemed as wise found themselves alone, braving the dust and animosity. Councillor Flyte turned a corner of the winding streets, ducking sharply to avoid an obscure metal fence railing that protruded from the eaves of a squat house. Stepping into a junction of several lanes, he raised his cassock sleeve to shield his eyes as the ripping wind hurled dust and wood shavings at him.

As the gust died away something larger, firmer struck him on the side of the head. Looking up from his cowered position, Flyte watched a small group of men materialise from the distorted street ahead. Normal men, average men, but bearing the menace of a pack of wolves.

"So, you've come down to slum it with the rest of us, have you?" one voice called out.

"I've come to offer s—" Flyte began.

"Don't!" he was interrupted. "Don't even try. It is insulting. Your very presence here is an insult. You and your so-called Wise Council needs to leave this city, broken as it is, behind."

"Look, I'm sure—" But another stone struck Flyte just below the eye and he buckled, clutching his face. The mob, growing in number, stepped forward as one.

"Please," Flyte pleaded, "we just came here to help."

"No you didn't," sneered a man with sand-smudged skin and hair matted to his forehead. "You saw us as simple, naïve folk and you thought you could take advantage." He kicked dust up into the councilman's squinting, bleeding face.

"Arrgghh! You savage!" he yelled, anger and loathing flaring up inside. "You're all imbeciles! Simpletons! Inbred cretins! You wouldn't know wh—" His voice was viciously silenced by the crashing blow of a metal rod.

*   *   *

Laurent's face was slashed with thorned scratches and stained with muddied tear tracks. There was no direction to his flight, merely a guilt-ridden fumbling from one gnarled tree trunk to the next, punctuated by self-pitying sobs. Everywhere he looked he saw her. All his memories of her replayed in his stream of consciousness. Their many walks in these woods now rotted to a wintery death knell. And he the executioner. His fingers clutched the crevices in the bark as bile burnt his throat and dripped from his lips to the earth. Falling to all fours, his body unable to support the weight of guilt, he crawled like a beast to the next knotted tree root at the base of a creepered tree. No longer human. But not of the forest. He belonged in some other place. Somewhere dark and twisted.

Reaching up, his briar-torn hand groped at a vine, which remained strong as he pulled himself to his feet. It took his weight as he hung from it, his body swaying and sagging, rendered immovable by the sheer burden of his own guilt. He was done. Could go no further. He no longer saw the forest around him.

Ivy.

Taking the vine, Laurent stared at it. Understood what

it offered him. Summoning enough strength, he wrapped the vine around his neck.

Ivy.

Coiled twice as he got to his knees. His breathing tightened. Hurt, he thought, but dulled by his own inner pain. Veins in his eyes starting to burst. Bloodshot.

Ivy.

Leaning into the truth.

Ivy.

*   *   *

By the time the mob reached the old Market Square, the numbers had swelled to a crowd, carrying the limp, blood strewn body of the councilman flung over their shoulders. Under the gathering blackened clouds they hoisted the prostrate figure atop a planted flagpole, crimson running down his face and staining his linen cloth tunic. A sweaty, dust-soaked resident turned, looking back over the deformed once-natural buildings and their avenues and alleyways.

"See this, you hideous carrion," he called out to the city streets, knowing the remaining council hid within. "You are not welcome here." His voice carried, reverberating off metal and mud. "We are taking back our city!" His victim, hanging by the scruff of his neck, groaned, and instinctively the speaker, bit between his teeth, lashed back out with the metal pole. It hit the defenceless councilman's leg with a crunch. Bystanders flinched; some cheered. The metal baton remained raised, poised.

"Stop!" croaked a voice from the murky mist. Cautiously inching forward from an avenue, three more elderly men came, one with his hands aloft in defence.

"We are unarmed. We mean you no harm…" The wizened voice trailed off as the murderous eyes of Fenwood turned to him, turned on him.

"No harm?" the pole-bearing figure hounded him. "No harm?! All you have done is cause harm! And now you expect us to shelter you? To comfort you? You… You have created this"—he gestured his arms widely—"this wildness. This madness." The crowd edged closer to the now cowering men. "It is time we embraced this chaos. Tear it all apart." And as if by some call of the wild, the mass of people took up the chant:

Tear it apart. Tear it apart."

The councilmen were grabbed, accosted, dragged into the throng, their cries drowned by the ferocious chorus.

"Tear it apart. Tear it apart."

The vitriol spilled into the streets, ripping away the metallic sheets, iron poles; anything that symbolised the lies, the false security, the betrayal.

"Tear it apart. Tear it apart."

The clanging of metal hitting the ground. Thuds of fists being thrown. The lust of violence.

"Tear it apart. Tear it apart."

In that moment, the frenzy threatened to destroy everything that had ever been, to fulfil the fears by their own selves.

"Tear. Tear. Tear."

And then…

They felt her arrival. A sensation. A glow. Her presence broke the violent impulse. The Mother reborn. Weapons were dropped, grimaces softened as slow realisation dawned. Into the midst of the carnage stepped Ivy, and yet not Ivy; the girl had been washed away and here stood a queen. Serene. A vision of hope. With just two words she conquered their hearts.

"My people."

CHAPTER 18

THE CALL OF THE WILD

The council, bloodied, bruised, belittled, left Fenwood much like the city itself, a wreck of what they once were. They did not leave behind the same lasting, visceral memory as their former lynchpin, Rukmahl, but after the dust had settled, even a whispered mention of them would end conversations. Fenwood had survived, but whilst buildings could be rebuilt there were some scars that would never heal.

Queen Ivy was much that the people hoped for and needed. She was kind, fair, intelligent. She allowed time for her people to grieve before she began implementing the slow, careful steps of restoration; a collective effort that unified her people in faith once more. Yet whilst she garnered love and respect, Ivy did not give herself wholly to the people, remaining somewhat aloof. She was never given the title Mother, nor held in the same adored esteem as her mother had been.

The regeneration began with the removal of all iron, steel and other metalwork that had blighted the relationship with the natural world that Fenwood had been founded on. The dwellings and businesses were returned to their wooden beginnings, many needing reinforcements and, in some cases, rebuilding from the wood stores that themselves needed replenishing. It was no small task. The Fenwood inhabitants were physically and emotionally drained. Yet, now they had purpose, hope and, through their new queen, a sense of belonging once again. She would walk among them often, no airs or graces, but one of them. Her smile was wide and infectious. She would speak with people, encourage people, but never offer insight into her own life or feelings.

*　　　　　*　　　　　*

The sun was setting on another day. The colours of deep yellow, orange, and crimson warmed the stone path to the castle doors. Looking down, Ivy noticed that it had been freshly swept. As she brushed dust from her linen britches, a voice called out to her and, turning, she saw a lady hurrying up the path behind her. The radiant smile touched Ivy's heart and, even though the woman could not find any words, she handed her queen a small bunch of hand-picked, wildflowers before scuttling away. Ivy sniffed them and inhaled the memories they brought. Of the woodland, of freedom... of him.

For some weeks after the breaking of Fenwood, Egan had been Ivy's constant companion. So much intrigued him about Ivy's world and about this new version of her. His wide-eyed, childish outlook endeared him to those whom he encountered: the way he touched things to experience them, how everything seemed so wondrously new to him. Many times, the revelation in the lower castle corridors came back to Ivy. It troubled her. For so long she was captivated by everything that he was, but there was a whole person she did not know. Who was Egan? She had been enraptured by everything he had symbolised for her. Yet there was clearly a life before, a history, a past. Why was his name buried in the depths of the castle, like a forbidden secret? Was that even his real name or merely a role he now played? How had he been left to begin a new life in the forest? She knew he would not give her answers, as if that story caused him great pain. She feared that crossing that unspoken divide would push him away. And suddenly she thought of her mother, realising that this is how she must have felt looking across the formal dining table at a daughter who built up walls in order to break free. Only now could she see the irony. So she held back her questions.

Almost as if he felt her hesitancy, Egan began disappearing for a day, here and there, from time to time. On his return, Ivy would notice a greenish smudge, muddied palm or ripped sleeve. Always she knew. She saw it in his animalistic mannerism, in the way he flinched in confined spaces, and in the way his gaze increasingly fell on the world outside the windows. She knew he was torn; as was she. The bond she had begun building with the people of Fenwood was in its infancy and she could not break it now. There was a commitment there, a silent promise she had made to herself, to her mother, to her people. But he had no such commitment, and at times it felt like he was torturing himself by choosing to stay in this cage.

As the sun broke over the horizon, Ivy watched him at the morning table. With a look of something between fascination and ruination, he surveyed the various tureens and dishes laid out in front of him. He dipped his fingertips into several of the plates, licking them and screwing up his face in disgust, much to the annoyance of

Mrs Maltcross who lingered by the doorway. Next, he drew the knife, fork and spoon into his hands, holding them all like a toddler. Ivy smiled at how comical he looked, but this gave way to pity. He tentatively jabbed the chicken thigh with the spoon and then the fork, then frowned. Dropping the cutlery, he took up the meat in his fingers, still on the bone, and attacked it with his teeth, tearing the flesh away. Mrs Maltcross had seen enough and slunk from the room. Ivy's eyes welled with tears.

Then one morning, he was gone. The chair at the far end of the morning table remained empty. There was no one to link her arm on the walk into Fenwood. Ivy's spoon rattled in the soup bowl in the silence of the evening meal. As she undressed for bed that evening, she considered venturing out under cover of darkness to find him. But she did not. The deep sigh she emitted was one of resigned acceptance.

Life went on. Ivy continued to wear her smile during the many visits through the streets of Fenwood, offering solace, comfort and advice, but the people felt her distance despite the love they bore her. She was kind, gracious, and yet they could not help but feel that her true heart was elsewhere.

The Oak and Maize inn became once again a place of quiet enjoyment. The bodies and conversations at the long, wooden tables slowly fell away. Hops stood drying an ale tankard with a well-worn cloth, his melancholy smile punctuated only by the clang of cutlery on lonely plates. He had kept this shattered community together by offering them a place to be. However, Hops would, of course, never admit to this.

"Hops?" called out a gruff voice from a frail, elderly man in the corner. "Is there any more ham hock?"

The innkeeper returned a warm smile.

"I'll have a look for you, Fred." And he disappeared into the back room.

*   *   *

It was some weeks later that the young queen eventually stole away from the newly glistening castle, passing through the ornate gardens and solid oaks, out into the wilderness. The trees whispered to each other of her presence, some bowing to her simple, faint footsteps in adulation. Ivy felt somehow afraid and comforted all at once. Those forgotten feelings of calm, togetherness, freedom came flowing back, and she breathed in the spectrum of greens, yellows and reds illuminated in the moonlight. She relished the crunch of the debris beneath her feet. Soon enough she found her way to the centre of the Great Crossroads, each way disappearing off into the towering trees and the darkness of the night. Someone had replaced the old, worn signpost with a fine beech pole and freshly painted directions. Glancing around, the stone circle which held Rukmahl's demise still stood, a crumbling ruin. Ivy wandered over, kneeling at the perimeter and touching the cold stone, remembering the awful cries of that dark, savage night. That was a moment in Fenwood's history that would never be recorded. Shaking her head, Ivy paced back toward the post, but where she was headed now had no sign, no clear path, secreted from view.

The forest fell to a hush as it watched the fair maiden, whispering at her passing. As if in response, a breeze drifted through. A call from the Gods.

*   *   *

The pool was expecting her. It glistened with the reflections of a thousand stars, the softest of ripples from the sleepily colliding lilies emanating a lulling peace. Ivy stood for some time at the water's edge, remembering. The arms of the guarding trees closed in protectively around her, the vulnerable girl that had hidden herself in the guise of a strong woman. She felt its magic, its power, the light shining from the beautiful night-mirrored waters.

Kneeling, she closed her eyes as tears began to fall tenderly down her cheeks.

"Thank you," she breathed.

A warm breeze wrapped itself around her. As she opened her eyes again, she saw him. A crouched figure on the mossy bridge that spanned the back of the pool. He paused, but in the darkness of the night Ivy could not see if he looked her way, or whether he had seen her at all. She opened her mouth to call to him, yet closed it again. A pause. A moment. And then he scurried into the undergrowth. Ivy stood, bolt upright, peering into the silhouetted shapes of the night. But he was gone. For some time, she remained motionless, staring. Then, with dignity, she wiped dry her cheeks and tied her brown hair into a tight knot, before finding her path home.

The queen returned many times to the pool; often over the following months she would be seen on the woodland paths, sometimes glimpsed passing between the trees. It was not known where she was headed or why, and when asked by those who chose to enquire she would merely smile absently and wish them a good day. The pool itself flourished with her company, channelling divine natural power. Yet it could not reunite her with the boy. As months turned to years, Ivy's visits became reserved for memorial days. Sometimes she smiled, sometimes she cried. Always she touched the water, breathed in the air, spoke without uttering a word. Just a girl, not a queen.

As the days wore on, Ivy's presence became less frequent at the still waters' side of the silent pool and it seemed to the watching world that each day she aged. Ivy had constructed for herself a crude seat, a wooden stump (dragged with some effort from the remains of a petrified tree), at the open end of the pool, where she would gaze across the tranquil water. It was unclear whether she was waiting for the boy to return to her, or whether she tried to understand what had happened. Every now and again those delicate, slender hands spread over her stomach and her eyes seemed to look far beyond the scene in front of her. But he never returned, and the understanding she sought never came. Her heart, once beating with passion and life and love, beat now only because it could.

Eventually the visits diminished and ceased.

The pool remained. Times moved on. Towns and cities were built, inhabited, expanded. The metallic, manmade nightmare that Fenwood had faced became the world's reality. Businesses became greedy for money rather than providing for their communities and the needs of their people, looking further and further afield for development and opportunity. Fenwood was a fly caught in a web of tracks and roads, and as the trade routes altered, more people found the pool, visited it, and began to pass by. Whilst all remarked on its beauty, it began to fade, as if being looked at too much were enough to wipe away the unspoilt vision. Towns grew around the neighbouring area to house those people who came to be part of this simple, natural lifestyle. In doing so they unwittingly broke it down, tree by tree. New stories enveloped the pool: a murder; a king's private swimming pool; acid in the water to clean clothes. With each fable its powers turned to legend, legend to myth, and eventually passed out of living memory. Sadly, Fenwood fell to the unrelenting charge of time, lost to new worlds of roads, industry and spectacle. Committees and well-meaning groups sought to preserve the pool, building a look-out hut and maintaining the bridge and walkways, hoping to attract visitors. A sideshow. A cheap trick. But the pool no longer held people's attention. It fell once again to the care of Nature; those same boughs and branches curtaining the waters and preserving all that had gone before. The water remained. The trees remained. But time could not hold onto the pool's magic, or power. With time comes great change.

EPILOGUE

The silver Corsa turned from the dual carriageway straight onto the potholed, gravel car park, and was brought to a stop under the shade of the trees. A young man stepped out, locked the car and zipped up his hoodie against the late afternoon chill. The sun still shone, but down in the valley the wind picked at unsheltered bodies. Immediately he headed through the gap in the trees and followed the path along to a clearing.

Where once was a silent pool, now a basin of dried forest debris lay; the remnants of a forgotten dream. Gone now was the wooden shack jutting from the bank; gone now was the water that swallowed the sunlight. Gone was the beauty, and the magic, and the life.

The young man slowed as he entered the clearing, but only stopped when he had reached the bank, still reinforced against the memory of water. He looked out across the dried leaves and twigs, trying to catch a glimpse of stories he had experienced sixteen years before. Nothing. Nothing now remained but the memory of an awestruck child. Had it ever been as beautiful as he remembered it to be?

The car door unlocked with its usual click. A musty odour of forgotten, wet trainers leapt from the interior once the door had been opened, enough that the young man leaned on the side of the car.

"It's a shame, isn't it?" a wavering voice said. The young man looked up. An elderly lady stood under the shade of the trees.

"I'm sorry?" said the young man.

"I said it's a shame," the lady said with a smile, "that there's no water left."

"Yes, it is a pity."

"I've come to sit here for many, many years, since before you were born. I've watched this place change."

The young man looked at the lady, and a smile of remembrance spread across his face.

"I came here with my dad when I was a small boy. It's changed a lot since then." The smile was one of disappointment.

"Did he tell you of the girl?" The lady took a step

forward.

"Yes, the one who drowned here? Yeah, I heard about her."

This time it was the lady who smiled, but more to herself than to her companion.

"Yes," she muttered. "That's the one."

"I always believed there was more to this place though," laughed the young man, the glint of the boy in his eyes. The lady looked into those eyes.

"Yes," she said, unmoving. "I know exactly what you mean."

ABOUT THE AUTHOR

Richard has lived in Portishead with his wife and two sons for nine years, having previously lived and worked in London. He has been a secondary school English teacher for 18 years since completing his teacher training after graduating with a degree in English, Film and Drama from Reading University. A keen adventurer, film fanatic and avid sports fan, Richard enjoys devoting his time to his family, but has relished the opportunity to have his first book published. *The Pool* was an idea formed as a young man and he is proud that it is to be his debut novel.

Follow Richard on:

Facebook: www.facebook.com/people/Richard-Collis/100073389871524/

Instagram: @Rich_Collis_author